"What Are You Doing Here, Vicki?"

She'd never heard Caleb sound this harsh, this unwelcoming. His tone shot her confidence to pieces. She almost turned to leave, but she was here now. And if she could come this far, she could keep going. Their marriage needed her effort.

"You walked away without letting me explain, Caleb."

"What's there to explain?"

So much, she thought desperately. And she couldn't find the right words. "I didn't know," she whispered. "I didn't know you thought I didn't want you." For so long she'd controlled her response to his touch, believing he'd be repulsed.

"Now you do." But he didn't reach out to gather her in his arms as he had so many nights in the past. He just kept his distance.

Dear Reader,

Thanks for taking time out of your hectic life to pick up and enjoy a Silhouette Desire novel. We have six outstanding reads for you this month, beginning with the latest in our continuity series, THE ELLIOTTS. Anna DePalo's *Cause for Scandal* will thrill you with a story of a quiet twin who takes on her identical sister's persona and falls for a dynamic hero. Look for her sister to turn the tables next month.

The fabulous Kathie DeNosky wraps up her ILLEGITIMATE HEIRS trilogy with the not-to-be-missed *Betrothed for the Baby*—a compelling engagement-of-convenience story. We welcome back Mary Lynn Baxter to Silhouette Desire with *Totally Texan,* a sensual story with a Lone Star hero to drool over. WHAT HAPPENS IN VEGAS...is perhaps better left there unless you're the heroine of Katherine Garbera's *Her High-Stakes Affair*—she's about to make the biggest romantic wager of all.

Also this month are two stories of complex relationships. Cathleen Galitz's *A Splendid Obsession* delves into the romance between an ex-model with a tormented past and the hero who finds her all the inspiration he needs. And Nalini Singh's *Secrets in the Marriage Bed* finds a couple on the brink of separation with a reason to fight for their marriage thanks to a surprise pregnancy.

Here's hoping this month's selection of Silhouette Desire novels bring you all the enjoyment you crave.

Happy reading!

Melissa Jeglinski

Melissa Jeglinski
Senior Editor
Silhouette Desire

Please address questions and book requests to:
Silhouette Reader Service
U.S.: 3010 Walden Ave., P.O. Box 1325, Buffalo, NY 14269
Canadian: P.O. Box 609, Fort Erie, Ont. L2A 5X3

NALINI SINGH

Secrets in the Marriage Bed

Silhouette® Desire

Published by Silhouette Books
America's Publisher of Contemporary Romance

SILHOUETTE BOOKS

ISBN 0-373-76716-1

SECRETS IN THE MARRIAGE BED

NALINI SINGH

has always wanted to be a writer. Along the way to her dream, she obtained degrees in both the arts and law (because being a starving writer didn't appeal). After a short stint as a lawyer, she sold her first book and from that point, there was no going back. Now an escapee from the corporate world, she is looking forward to a lifetime of writing, interspersed with as much travel as possible. Currently residing in Japan, Nalini loves to hear from readers. You can contact her via the following e-mail address: nalini@nalinisingh.com; or by writing to her c/o Silhouette Books, 233 Broadway, Suite 1001, New York, NY, 10279, U.S.A.

This one's for all my readers—
you guys are the greatest.

One

"I'm pregnant."

Caleb Callaghan's heart rocked to a standstill. "What?"

"I said I'm pregnant. Three months along—the doctor just confirmed it." Shoving her fingers through her shoulder-length blond hair, Vicki sat down in the chair across from his desk.

His entire mind restarted with a kick—this was the chance he'd been waiting for, for two long months. He would not let it slip away. Rising, he moved around the desk to kneel beside her chair. "You're carrying our child." Wonder held him in its grip. Within the space of a few seconds, the hell of his life had turned into heaven.

Vicki can't divorce me if she's pregnant.

As if she'd heard him, she shook her head. "It doesn't change anything." But her voice held the tiniest hint of uncertainty.

He seized the moment. No way was he going to fight fair, not when this was the most important battle of his life. "Of course it does." He took her fine-boned hand, delighting in once again being able to touch her.

"No."

"Yes." In the months since their separation, he'd tried everything he could think of to win his wife back. And failed. But this, this would not allow Vicki to so easily justify a divorce. "How can it not change everything? That's *my* baby you're carrying."

Her hand tensed in his. "Don't bully me, Caleb."

Warned by her tone, he rapidly recalculated his approach. Though he had no intention of letting her shut him out any longer, he knew that if he pushed too hard, he might lose her. But his Victoria had always had a soft heart. "I have a right to experience this with you. This is my first baby, too. Maybe my last."

Emotions he had no hope of understanding flickered across her face at the speed of light. "You want to move back in," she said, referring to their restored villa above St. Marys Bay, not far from Auckland's city center.

"I *am* moving back in." That was non-negotiable. "I'm not letting you divorce me while our child is in your womb." That gave him six months in which to convince her that their marriage was worth saving, that five years of commitment shouldn't be thrown away so quickly.

She'd asked him for space when they'd separated and he'd given her that as far as he was able—limiting himself to a phone call a day and a couple of visits a week to ensure that she was okay. But that was all ending as of this moment. He wanted his wife back. "This baby is a gift, Vicki—our chance to make it. Don't throw that away."

Her eyes seemed to soften.

Standing, he tugged her up and into his embrace, her slender body a perfect fit against his larger frame. "I'll get my stuff delivered from the hotel this afternoon." He hated the damn place because it wasn't home, would never be home. "We'll be all right." He'd ensure it. No matter what, he wasn't going to lose her.

She was his everything.

Vicki let Caleb hold her and knew she was making a terrible mistake. But God, she'd missed being in her husband's arms. For two months she'd missed him every single day. Each time he'd invited her to lunch, each time he'd dropped by for coffee, she'd known she should back away but instead had always agreed. Now that dangerous pattern threatened to continue. "You don't need to be at home to share this with me."

He loosened his hold enough that she could look up into those hazel eyes, shades lighter than his dark brown hair. "Hell yes, I do. You want to raise our kid like you were raised? Barely knowing his—or her—father?"

She sucked in a breath. "You know exactly where to aim, don't you?" If there was one thing she didn't want, it was for their child to grow up feeling unloved by either parent.

Letting her go, he put his hands on his hips under his suit jacket. "I'm not going to sugarcoat the truth—if you insist on this separation, it's going to lead to divorce and eventually to a child shuttled from home to home."

"You think it's better for our baby to grow up in the middle of a battlefield?" She would not bring an innocent soul into the wreckage that was their marriage right now.

"Of course not." His voice rose. "But, Vicki, you can't have it both ways. Either you let me in and we start working on things, or you accept the alternative."

"This is moving too fast—I need time."

"You've had two months." His jaw was set. "More than enough time."

It was nowhere near enough, she thought. They'd seen each other several times a week during the separation but had yet to talk, really talk. "Caleb, look at it from my point of view. I just found out I'm pregnant. Having you back on top of that is going to be too much to cope with."

"And the longer you keep me away, the less time we'll have to fix things before the baby arrives," he responded. "I'm not backing down on this, so you might as well say yes."

If she hadn't already made her decision before walking into this firm that he'd built with sheer determination, his statement might have rubbed her raw. But though so much of him was a mystery to her, this she'd predicted. From the second she'd discovered her pregnancy—though she'd had every intention of trying to convince him otherwise—she'd known that Caleb would refuse to keep his distance.

With that in mind, she'd thought long and hard about the conditions under which she'd allow him to move back into the house. "All right." Even as she said those words, she was regretting them—give Caleb an inch and he'd take a mile. But this was no longer just about the two of them.

"That's the right decision, honey," he said. "You'll see. We'll be okay."

Frowning at his tone, she started to point out that things were going to be a little different this time around. "Look, you can move in, but—"

"Sh." He smiled and put his hand on her abdomen, startling her with the gesture. It made her pregnancy feel real in a way that even the doctor's announcement hadn't. "Don't want the kid to hear us arguing, do you?"

Her stomach twisted. Already, it was starting—she spoke and he didn't listen. "Caleb, I want to tell you—"

"Later." He raised his hand to push her hair off her face. "We have all the time in the world."

All his things were in the guest bedroom.

"What the hell is this?" Caleb turned to find his wife standing in the bedroom doorway, arms folded and eyes narrowed. No trace remained of the woman who'd let him hold her only a few hours ago.

Straightening her spine, she met his challenge head-on. "This is you not listening—you steamrolling over my objections to your moving back in just as you steamroll over everything." There was steel in that soft voice he was used to hearing murmur in agreement.

"Later, you said. Well, this is 'later.' You can stay in the house but don't expect to move back into my life like nothing ever happened. As far as I'm concerned, we're still separated."

He froze, shock acting like a narcotic in his blood. In the five years they'd been married, Vicki had *never* spoken to him like that. "Sweetheart—"

"No. No, Caleb. I'm not letting you push me into something I'm not ready for."

"This isn't giving us a chance," he argued. "We can hardly work on our problems if I'm banished to this room with you holding the threat of divorce over my head." Throwing his suit jacket on the bed, he began to tear off his tie, his eyes on Vicki.

"Neither is your way." Her cheeks flushed with temper. "You want everything to go back to what it was—as if you haven't been living in a hotel for the past two months... I was miserable in our marriage. Is that the wife you want back?"

Her words hurt. "You never said *anything* and then one day, you tell me you want a divorce. How the hell was I supposed to know you weren't happy? I'm not a mind reader." Giving up on the blasted tie, he shoved a hand through his hair.

Vicki clenched her fists, creamy skin taut over delicate bones. "No," she said. "You're not. But you wouldn't have to be if you occasionally took the time to listen to me instead of insisting on your way or no way."

Caleb was getting good and mad. "You never wanted to make any decisions so I made them." Since the day he'd married her, he'd done his best to take care of her, protect her, and this was his thanks?

"Did you ever stop to think I might want more from life than to call you lord and master? People grow and change, Caleb. Didn't you ever consider that I might have?"

Her sharp question brought his growing temper to a screeching halt, because the truth was, in his mind Vicki had remained the poised but still young bride of nineteen he'd carried into his home five years ago. Given the gap in their ages and life experiences, his taking charge of their marriage had been inevitable.

That wasn't to say she'd been lacking her own strengths. In fact, she'd been unnaturally mature for her age, completely willing and able to take over her role as the wife of an ambitious young litigator determined to become better than the best.

He wouldn't have been drawn to her if he hadn't glimpsed the resilient will behind her shy smiles. But while he'd already walked a hard road by the age of twenty-nine, she'd been untested by the world, cocooned in an environment where everyone behaved according to accepted rules. Used to making decisions, it hadn't occurred to him to act any other way with his wife.

For the first time in a long while, he looked at her without being blinded by memories of the girl she'd been. She was still slender, still beautiful in that graceful way with her blue eyes and that silky hair he loved to have brush over his skin. But her eyes no longer said what they had in the past.

When they'd wed, she'd looked to him for everything. Now…now there was distance in those blue depths, a world of secrets he was shut out of. To his shock, he found he had no idea who she was behind her elegant shell.

"No, I guess I didn't." He'd built his life around his self-confidence, trusting his instincts when there'd been nothing and no one else to trust. To admit he'd been wrong about something this important was a blow.

Vicki's lips parted, her eyes going wide.

"But don't blame me for everything," he continued. They'd both been in that broken marriage and if they were going to survive the rebuilding, they had to be honest. "You know what I'm like. If you'd said something, I would have tried to fix it. I don't like to see you hurting."

Which was why he'd never berated her for the one thing she couldn't give him—her passion, her desire. That absence in their marriage had stung like hell, and still did, but he was incapable of harming her, even to assuage his own pain. From the moment he'd met her, all he'd wanted to do was make her happy…make her smile.

Shoulders taut beneath the white linen of her simple shift dress, she shook her head. "That's the point, Caleb. I don't want you to fix things for me. I need…"

"What, Vicki? Tell me what you need." It was something he'd never asked. The realization stunned him, made him question exactly how good a job he'd done of loving her.

Even in bed, he'd taken the lead, confident in his ability to ensure her physical pleasure though he couldn't make her want him with the fury that he wanted her. But what if she'd needed something else, something he hadn't known how to give? What if that was the reason she'd never responded to him with the intensity he needed from her?

Her whole face softened. "I just need you to see and love *me,* not the idea of the perfect wife you have in your head, or the woman Grandmother tried to mold me into. Just me. Just Victoria."

It felt as if she'd struck him. "I never tried to change you."

"No, Caleb. You never even saw me at all." And that had hurt more than anything. Because no matter what she said and did, she loved Caleb Callaghan with every breath in her body. Loved his laugh, his intelligence, his stubbornness and even his temper.

But it wasn't enough. Love like that could slowly destroy a person from the inside out if it wasn't returned. And despite what Caleb believed, she knew it wasn't. To her husband she was as fragile as an exotic bloom, someone who always had to be protected, even if that meant she had to be shielded from the full power of his own feelings.

Like now. His fists were clenched, his jaw taut but he kept himself under control. "If I didn't see you, then who the hell did I spend five years with? A ghost?"

The sarcastic comment fell too close to the mark. "Maybe you did."

"What's that supposed to mean?"

How did she tell him something she'd barely started to understand herself? "Who was I in that marriage, Caleb?"

"My *wife*." His hazel eyes were clouded with a kind of pain she'd never before seen. "Wasn't that enough?"

"Caleb Callaghan's wife," she said, swallowing the knot of emotion in her throat. "But was I really even that?"

He scowled. "What kind of question is that? Of course you were my wife. You still are. And if you'd get over this separate-bedrooms crap, we could start working on making things right."

If I'm your wife, she wanted to scream, *then why did you do* that *with Miranda?* But that wasn't something she was strong enough to face yet—four months of distance from the event hadn't even formed a scab on the wound. "This is not crap, Caleb. This is real, so start paying attention—for once in your life, pay attention to your marriage!"

Swiveling on her heel, she walked out of the room. From behind her came the harsh sounds of Caleb swearing and throwing something at the wall, but he didn't follow her. Relieved, she entered her own room, knowing she was close to an emotional meltdown. It was one thing to coach herself on how to handle Caleb when it was only hypothetical, and quite another to be faced with the full force of his personality.

She'd spent her marriage unable to say what needed to be said because she'd been too weak to stand up to the force of nature that was Caleb Callaghan. Having him home scared her—what if she crumpled again, losing everything she'd gained in the months they'd been apart, months in which she'd made herself take a critical look at her life?

What she'd seen hadn't been pretty. But at least she was

facing her mistakes now, facing the mess of their marriage. Getting Caleb to do the same would be a major battle, but she'd made a beginning two months ago when she'd gambled everything on a throw of the dice and asked him for a divorce.

It had been a move born of desperation and staked on Caleb's stubborn refusal to admit defeat in any arena. She'd wanted to shake him out of his complacency, to make him see that the life they'd been living wasn't a life at all, merely an existence. Despite her hurt over what he'd done with Miranda during that business trip to Wellington, she hadn't wanted to give up on the dream that had first brought them together.

But not even for that dream had she been willing to continue hiding behind the perfect facade of their fractured marriage. So she'd thrown the dice. And waited for Caleb to pick them up.

He hadn't let her down. Though he'd moved out, he'd made sure he had contact with her almost every day. Now, the unexpected gift of their baby had given them more time, time enough for Caleb to get to know her, to begin to understand the woman she'd always been beneath the brittle shell of breeding and culture.

After he understood who she was, he'd have to decide whether or not he wanted to remain married to her, whether or not he wanted to fight to fix a marriage she wasn't sure could be fixed. Vicki had no intention of ever again donning the mask of a fashion-conscious socialite wife. The question was, what if that was exactly the kind of woman Caleb wanted?

A woman who'd go her own way and not demand anything from him but money and a place in society; a woman who'd turn the other cheek when infidelity raised its ugly head; a woman who'd never dream of destroying her upper-class lifestyle by divorcing her husband because he didn't love her.

Two

Caleb was in a foul mood. He'd fully expected to spend the night with his wife, but instead had tossed and turned in the guest bedroom while Vicki lay feet away. By the time the shrill ring of the alarm woke him, all of his nerves had been rubbed raw.

He didn't understand why Vicki was doing this to them—she'd never acted so unreasonably before. How could she expect them to pretend to be separated when they were both living in the same house and she was about to have his baby, for God's sake? As far as he was concerned, separate beds were not part of the marriage deal. And he'd missed her, damn it. Hadn't she missed him even a bit?

After a quick shower, he pulled on his suit jacket and walked into the kitchen, expecting a cold welcome from the woman he'd spent the night dreaming about. Vicki stood at the counter pouring coffee into his cup. His mood elevated. "I half expected you to tell me to fend for my-self." That was what she'd done in the last weeks before their separation.

She rolled her eyes. "If I didn't feed you, you'd live on takeout."

He slid onto a stool on the other side of the counter, lux-uriating in the feel of being home again. In spite of the hours he'd worked as a rising young lawyer, he'd restored this villa with his own hands. It had been his escape from the combative world in which he spent much of his life.

When he'd married Vicki, the villa had only been par-tially restored and he'd expected her to balk at the work remaining, but she'd lit up at the prospect. She'd done a lot of the finishing work herself—he'd often come home to a wife with paint-stained skin and scraped knuckles.

Almost a year later, they'd had a bright, airy home stamped with their personalities. Some of the happiest days of their marriage had been spent covered in paint and sawdust, with only each other's voices for company.

"Do vending-machine snacks count as proper food?" he asked, trying to tease his way back into their normal routine. The separation had been hell—he had no inten-tion of returning to that empty existence, no matter what he had to do to convince Vicki.

She gave him an arch look and broke a couple of eggs into a bowl. "I hope you're joking."

Caleb knew how to cook. Forced by circumstance, he'd learned to do so as a young child, feeding both himself and his younger sister when his parents became too caught up in themselves. But from the first day of their marriage, Vicki had taken over the kitchen and he'd let her. It had always been one of his secret pleasures that his wife cared enough about him to ensure he ate properly. No one else had ever bothered.

Which was why it had hurt so much when she'd stopped.

Taking the coffee, along with the plate of scrambled eggs and bacon she passed over, he tried out a smile. "Aren't you joining me?" Breakfast was one of the few meals they'd managed to share regularly. He wondered what she'd do if she knew that he'd skipped breakfast while living at the hotel, unable to bear her absence. Not that he had any intention of telling her.

She made a face. "I think I'll wait an hour or so."

"You okay, sweetheart?"

Her lips curved into a smile that sucker punched him with its beauty. "Just a tiny bit of morning sickness that's actually hitting in the morning, for once."

"Doesn't it always?" He was fascinated by the life growing inside of her, hoped she wouldn't shut him out of the experience the way she'd shut him out of her bed.

She shook her head. "No. It comes and goes on its own schedule. But I'm lucky—I haven't really had it bad at all. Eat or you'll be late."

Obeying, he watched her move around the kitchen dressed in jeans and a sea-green cardigan that looked so touchable, he wondered if she'd worn it to torment him. His hands itched to mold themselves over her slender frame. Her three-month-old pregnancy wasn't yet visible and she looked much as she'd done when they'd married, but as he'd learned last night, things had changed.

"Toast." She plucked two pieces out of the toaster, buttered them and handed them over.

As he took them, his gaze fell on a pale pink envelope sitting on the far end of the counter next to the fruit bowl. "What's that?"

"A card from Mother."

He eyed her carefully. "What does it say?"

"Only that she might be visiting Auckland in a week or two to catch up with me. Eat." She waved a hand at him and walked over to put the envelope in the back pocket of her jeans.

Caleb wondered if she really felt as carefree as she was making out. Danica Wentworth's infrequent interruptions of Vicki's life tended to leave his wife distraught. He'd tried to broach the subject with her more than once, but she'd backed away with alacrity that spoke of such deep pain, he'd never pursued it. In truth, part of him worried that if he pushed her on this point, she might push back, and there were things about his childhood he wanted no one to know.

But that same childhood had also given him the tools to understand her wariness. What child would want to remember the woman who'd abandoned her to pursue a lover? Though that man had gone on to marry another, Danica remained in a relationship with him to this day—she'd never left him like she'd left her four-year-old daughter. Worse, she had entrusted Vicki to her ex-husband's mother, Ada, a woman about as maternal as a gutter snake.

Vicki shot him a curious look when he continued to stare at her. "What?"

"Nothing." Nothing that he could put into words.

He ached to walk over and wrap her in his arms, to *show* her what he felt. It seemed as though he'd spent eternity aching to hold his wife. But always he stopped, knowing that she wouldn't welcome such advances. That moment in his office yesterday had been an aberration. She'd been upset and vulnerable and he'd acted on instinct.

"Are you going to court today?" She eyed his black suit and to his surprise, came over to fix the collar of his shirt. The woman-scent of her went straight to his heart.

He nodded, trying not to look as stunned as he felt. Vicki never touched him unless he initiated contact. "The Dixon-McDonald case."

Her eyes met his and she dropped her hands, as if startled by her own actions. "Two companies fighting it out over a patent, right?" A soft blush shading her cheeks, she walked around the counter and picked up the carafe to refill his coffee. "Think you guys will win?"

He was further surprised by her knowledge of the case. "Callaghan & Associates always win." He grinned despite feeling strangely off balance. Vicki was…different.

Though she refused to meet his gaze, she laughed. "What's the firm doing involved in a patent case? I thought that was pretty specialized."

God, he'd missed her laugh. It made him realize how long it had been since he'd heard it—months before his move to the hotel. "When did you start keeping track of my files?" His tone was conversational but in his gut, guilt churned. Why hadn't he noticed the extent of her unhappiness before now? Even when she'd rocked their world by asking him for a divorce, he hadn't woken up to that fact. Why the hell not? Had he been so wrapped up in work he'd forgotten the woman he'd promised to love, honor and cherish?

Finally, she raised her head. "Since always."

"But you've never talked to me about any of them before." Never talked about the firm he'd built with blood, sweat and tears, though it had been an integral part of their life. "Even when you held dinner parties for my clients, you asked barely enough to ensure things ran smoothly."

"I…" She paused and then took a deep breath. "I guess I didn't want to sound stupid. It's not like I have legal or corporate training. And you never seemed to want to discuss your work when you came home. I thought maybe it had something to do with confidentiality."

His head spun at the uncertainty in her tone. "You couldn't sound stupid if you tried. Attorney-client privilege doesn't stop us discussing things in general terms like we just did. I never talked about work because I thought you weren't interested." And why exactly had he thought that?

The answer remained frustratingly out of reach, but he understood enough to fix this mistake. "The reason we got involved is that the client followed Marsha Henrikkson—" he named one of his newer associates "—when she switched to our firm. She's a qualified patent attorney."

Vicki beamed at him.

"What?" he asked, rocked by his own pleasure at having made his wife smile. Sunlight shimmered off the wooden counter and suddenly, bittersweet shards of memory cut into him. He remembered sanding this counter and looking up to find Vicki smiling at him from the other side. Back then he'd been full of hope for their future, still cocky enough to laughingly grab his wife and tumble her to the floor.

"Nothing." Continuing to smile, she asked, "Do you want more toast?"

Memory and reality converged in her happiness. "No, this will hold me." He took a last sip of coffee and stood, wishing he didn't have an early appointment. The two of them hadn't been this easy with each other for far too long. "I'll call if I'm going to be late."

"Fine."

He caught the edge in her tone. "What does that mean?" If blunt questions were what it would take for him to get to know this intriguing woman who'd shown him more fire and passion in one day than she had during the rest of their marriage, he'd ask a thousand of them.

Her jaw firmed. "You're always late, Caleb. I can't remember the last time we had dinner together when it wasn't a work function."

He'd never thought she cared one way or the other if he was around. After all, she could hardly bear it when he reached for her and if he was with her, he wanted to touch her. Her dislike of intimacy with him had half destroyed him, but she was still the only woman he wanted as his wife. "You want me home for dinner?"

"Of course I want you home for dinner!" Frown lines marred her forehead. "You're my husband."

The decision was easy. "I'll be home."

Another unexpected smile lit up her features, erasing the frown. "Really?"

"Promise." He wanted nothing more than to kiss her and taste the sunshine sparkling on her lips.

She stepped closer. "I'll wait for you."

He wished she'd touch him, hug him, anything. But Vicki had never taken that sort of action and eventually, he'd learned to withhold his own inherently physical nature, learned not to ask for things she could never give him.

Even if it shredded his soul.

Vicki watched Caleb get into his dark sedan and drive away. No matter how well she thought she knew him, he could always surprise her. The way he'd agreed to come home early without any hesitation had been a shock, given his dedication to his work.

She *hated* coming second to the law firm that was his life, hated it with a vengeance that could have turned her bitter if she hadn't decided to do something about it. Caleb's easy acquiescence to her request gave her hope that the battle might not be as impossible as it had always seemed. Maybe he was listening to her at long last.

But, she thought suddenly, was she listening to him? There had been something in his eyes as he'd looked at her in the kitchen—as if he'd wanted to say something, do something, but was restraining himself. She got that impression a lot around Caleb. Restraint. Emotions held captive.

He hadn't started out that way. In the beginning, she'd almost drowned in the power of Caleb, a little frightened at the strength of his focus on her but delighting in it all the same. Then something had changed between them…been damaged.

If she'd walked over to fix his collar when they'd first married, no matter how angry they were with each other, he would have pulled her into his lap and kissed her until she begged for mercy. She'd touched him deliberately this morning as a test to see how much remained of that early passion. The answer had devastated her.

What had happened to the fire that had once raged between them? Had she destroyed it? She didn't know what to think, experience warring with childhood lessons about acceptable behavior and the need to control her emotions. All she knew was that she'd die if she was never again as important to Caleb as she'd been at the start.

But why then did she get the impression that Caleb was constantly fighting to rein in his nature? Why could she almost *feel* the dark intensity of the emotions he kept locked up? And why could she never ask him what it was that he wanted to say but didn't?

He was right. He hadn't been the only one who'd made mistakes in their marriage.

Three

Caleb arrived home that evening to find Vicki in the living room staring at the phone. Dressed in a sleeveless black dress that faithfully hugged every curve, she looked tempting enough to eat. His gut clenched at the thought that she'd donned a sexy dress for dinner. What the hell was that supposed to mean?

"Anything the matter?" Dropping his briefcase on the couch, he stripped off his overcoat and suit jacket. Autumn was turning into winter and the breeze coming off the bay was increasingly crisp. But it was warm inside the house, the sunlight trapped by both the windows and the skylights.

"Your secretary just called from her apartment. She said she forgot to tell you she'd managed to reschedule with Mr. Johnson. The meeting is now at eight tomorrow morning."

That was the appointment Caleb had cancelled in order to be home for dinner. "Thanks for taking the message. My mobile's dead—I forgot to charge it." Tugging off his tie, he dropped it on the sofa before undoing the top two buttons of his shirt and walking over to join her. "Why the look?" The urge to run his hands over the delicate softness of her bare arms was a physical ache.

"It wasn't Miranda," she blurted out, troubled eyes looking to him for explanation.

If there was one thing he didn't want to discuss, it was his former secretary. "No. She's been gone awhile." Giving in to temptation, he curved one hand over the creamy skin of her shoulder. She shivered but didn't move away. Then again, she never did. At least not until the end.

Victoria wanted to ask why Miranda had left but the courage that had pushed her this far deserted her in the face of the sickening thought that bloomed in her mind without warning. What if Miranda was no longer Caleb's secretary because she was something else? Such arrangements weren't unheard of in the circles in which she'd grown up—her own mother was a perfect example. And Caleb had been living away from her for two months. Maybe he'd gotten tired of waiting.

"Vicki?"

The reply she wanted to make kept slipping out of the turmoil in her mind. She stared at the floor in a desperate attempt to find her sense of balance but suddenly her world was spinning. "I need to sit…" And then it was too much effort to speak.

She heard him swear. Before she could collapse, he scooped her up in those powerful arms and she felt herself being carried to the sofa. He sat down with her held close. "Vicki? Talk to me. Come on, sweetheart."

She took several deep breaths, letting herself be comforted by the only man who'd ever given her this tenderness. "I'm okay. Just give me a moment."

"Are you sick? Is something wrong with the baby?" he demanded.

"No, no. I'm fine. We're both fine." Realizing that strands of hair were escaping her carefully constructed coil, she lifted her hand to re-anchor the pins. Caleb's eyes drifted up.

And she remembered.

Instead of fixing the elegant do, she pulled out the pins and let the soft mass fall around her shoulders. Caleb had always loved it when she wore her hair loose, though he'd never once said so out loud. Some things a wife simply knew.

"If you're both okay, why did you faint?"

Because I just realized that you might have a mistress. Held in fear's tight grip, she didn't speak the words. She may have become stronger in recent months, but she wasn't strong enough to hear his response to that statement. Not yet. As long as she didn't say it, Caleb couldn't lie to her, couldn't fracture the fragility of their new start.

"I think I overdid it making dinner," she said, with a small shrug. "I should've sat down a bit more during the day." A lie of omission hidden in truth.

"Are you sure that's all?" His hand drifted to her nape, a soft massage that was all the more seductive because of his overwhelming physicality. As usual, his touch made her want to behave in ways that were utterly unladylike and vaguely terrifying.

Did he do this for Miranda? *Stop it!* she told herself the second the thought entered her mind. She wouldn't let her own fears and suspicions sabotage the decision she'd made with her eyes wide open.

In their time apart, despite all her hurt and anger, she'd accepted that she loved Caleb in a way that was so deep, it was a once-in-a-lifetime gift. Though that realization had spurred her to fight for their marriage, it wouldn't stop her from walking away if they failed. And if she kept letting the past interfere, they would surely fail. For the sake of their child, she had to look beyond Caleb's relationship with Miranda.

"Vicki? Come back to me, honey. Is everything really okay?"

She started to nod but her mouth shaped the word "no." And she knew that although there was one wound she might never be ready to talk about, it was time to lay open another. "I spent a lot of time thinking about us today."

Those hazel eyes seemed to harden but he didn't stop his massage. "What's to think about? We're married and you're carrying our child."

"No, Caleb. Don't do this again. Listen to me."

"Talk."

"You were angry about the separate beds last night." But not angry enough to go elsewhere, she told herself, trying to soothe the agony in her heart.

"I want my wife in my bed. What's wrong with that?"

"But that bed wasn't the happiest of places for us, was it? I wasn't ever…woman enough for you. I could never satisfy you." It was like ripping out pieces of her soul and handing them over to him, but this had to be done.

"Jesus, Vicki."

"You know I'm right, Caleb." No matter how humiliating it was for her to admit…to accept, her failure in bed had helped drive him into another woman's arms. If Vicki wanted Caleb back, she had to face up to that.

Caleb didn't know what to do. He was used to taking charge but, at that moment, he was lost. Stroking her cheek, he shook his head. "Don't look so sad, sweetheart."

Many times in the last few years of their marriage, he'd glimpsed that haunting sadness in her expression.

He'd felt helpless that he couldn't bring the light he'd caught tantalizing glimpses of before they'd married back into her eyes. He'd assumed that once she was out from under her grandmother's shadow, the light would flare bright, but it had faded until he'd been terrified he'd done something to kill it. "It's nothing that we can't fix."

"Do you really think so?"

"Yes, Vicki. *Yes*. But we can't do it if you won't let me into your bed." When she didn't respond, he tried another approach. "We're going in with a new mind-set—it changes everything."

"Yes, it has to, doesn't it?" Nodding in agreement, she wrapped her arms around his neck and lay her head against his shoulder. "Oh, Caleb. I missed having you beside me."

He'd loved her long enough to understand the message in the liquid softness of her body. *Please, don't let me be deceiving myself.* This was as close as Vicki ever came to making the first move. Sure that he was reading her right, he stood and, with her in his arms, headed for the bedroom. When she held on tighter, the knot in his chest eased.

Maybe it would be different now that they'd finally brought the secret pain of their marriage out into the open. Maybe Vicki would respond to him in the way he'd always wanted her to respond. Maybe.

She didn't say a word as he carried her into the master bedroom. When he set her on her feet, they just looked at each other for several long seconds, two starving people in front of a banquet. The same moment that he began to reach for her, Vicki's lashes fluttered shut and her body swayed toward his.

Cupping her face, he kissed her. She always responded

to this, kissing him back with explosive passion. He cherished the kisses she gave him during lovemaking because they were the only signs that she wanted him.

So he kissed her. For a long, long time. Kissed…and hoped. When she whimpered and made a small restless movement, he slid his hands to the back of her dress and pulled down the zipper. Trailing his fingers up her spine, he became fascinated by the delicacy of her skin but resisted the urge to linger. Part of him was afraid this moment would be lost if he didn't hurry. Promising himself he could return to savor her, he raised his hands to the shoulders of the dress and slid them down her arms. She let go of him only for the instant it took to remove the dress from her upper body.

The sound of cloth on skin sizzled over him as the dress fell to puddle around her bare feet. The feel of her almost naked body was an erotic shock. Exquisitely shaped, her breasts were small, taut, letting her eschew a bra when she chose…like tonight. He loved when she did that. It drove him half crazy.

Still kissing her, he moved his hands down her sides, stopping to stroke his thumbs over her nipples. She gasped into the kiss but didn't react in any other way. Her hands didn't move from around his neck; her body didn't press closer to his. Caleb didn't give up. She'd raised the topic, welcomed his embrace. What clearer indication of desire did he need?

He shed his shirt without breaking the kiss, then hesitantly pressed their bodies together. Her breasts rubbed against his chest, a sweet kind of torture. There was no rejection in her body, but neither could he read *true* welcome, passionate need. Only her mouth gave him hope.

Breaking the kiss at last, he lifted her and put her on

the bed. Wide, the design a simple wooden frame, they'd picked it out in the weeks before their marriage, never guessing that it would become the center of one of the major issues in their relationship.

His hands trembled as he tugged her panties down her thighs, two months of deprivation making him ravenous. She was the most beautiful woman he'd ever seen and all he wanted to do was lavish his attention on every part of her, to take his time and adore her inch by precious inch. But such slow, luxurious loving required more than co-operation. Nothing less than acceptance on the deepest, most intimate level would do. And even tonight, Vicki held him at a distance, her desire locked up tight.

For five years he'd made love to her as little as possible, needing her more than he needed to breathe but unwilling to hurt her with his demands. Her kisses were always pure fire, her body slick and ready whenever he entered her, but in between, she never responded, no matter how hard he tried.

It didn't matter that he could always bring her to orgasm. What mattered was that she fought every pleasure he tried to give her. What mattered was that she was never so overcome by desire that she became ravenous for *him*. What mattered was that even in this most personal of situations, his wife refused to drop her shield of cool elegance.

Hoping against hope, he kicked off his shoes and lowered himself on top of her, bracing himself on his arms. As his lips claimed hers, he ran one hand down her body to cup her buttock, and touched her hand.

It was clenched into a fist.

Four

A sound of raw pain ripped out from somewhere deep inside him as he rolled away. "Shit." He wasn't going to do this if she was merely enduring the experience. At least before the separation, she'd held on to him as if she'd never let go, allowing him to fool himself into thinking that she wanted him. But this...no more. Something in him had given way, broken. After all this time, he'd hit his own limits.

He heard her move, thought he heard muffled sobs as she got under the sheets. The knife inside him twisted and twisted until he wondered if he was bleeding. Shoving his hands through his hair, he laid on his back and stared at the ceiling, fighting the emotions threatening to take control. He wasn't sure he could cope with that much pain. After several minutes, he shifted to look at her. She was lying on her side, giving him her back.

He thought about the number of times she'd turned

away from him in bed. The broken part of him was suddenly furious. "Why did you marry me if you can't stand my touch?" That fact had tormented him for years. At first he'd hoped that nothing more than shyness kept her from touching him, but he had slowly realized that it was something far worse.

His wife didn't want him.

Devastated, he'd tried to limit his earthy sexuality, tried not to burden her with his need. And yet he hadn't been able to stop himself from reaching for her in the darkness, when his shields were at their lowest and he could no longer fight the hunger. Today she'd ripped those shields completely from him, taunting him with a false hope that things would be different. Why had she done that?

Vicki's back stiffened and she faced him, something like shock in her eyes. "I love the way you touch me."

He let out a harsh bark of laughter. "Yeah, right. That's why when we have sex, you can't wait for me to finish so you can roll away and pretend you didn't let me put my hands on you."

Unable to make her see what she was doing to him, he'd focused the frustrated power of his emotions on his work. Combined with his inherent need to succeed, to prove himself, he'd been unstoppable. In five years he'd achieved more with the firm than many men did in a lifetime. No one knew that his phenomenal success had come at the cost of denying the passion at the core of him.

Vicki shook his shoulder, forcing him to look at her. Her eyes were cloudy with distress. "No, Caleb! That's not true. I never—I adore making love with you."

She'd started this but if she wasn't prepared to admit to the depth of their problems, he could see no way out. He sat up. "I'm going for a drive." His voice was ragged, his arousal fading under the accumulated weight of years of rejection. Grabbing his shirt, he shoved his arms into the sleeves and started to walk out.

"Caleb, wait!"

Pretending he hadn't heard, he continued walking away. He couldn't bear to let her see him like this, vulnerable, wounded and so hurt he could barely find his way out of the room.

Victoria gave up trying to fall asleep sometime around two in the morning. Though Caleb had long since returned, they never did have that dinner she'd dressed up for with such high hopes. Like so many other meals in the past, it had fallen by the wayside. Except this time it wasn't Caleb's work at fault but her own cowardice.

Lying on her back, she stared at the darkness of the ceiling through tear-filled eyes and thought about the mess she'd made of her life. It was no use continuing to blame Caleb for the field of broken dreams that had become their marriage, no matter how easy that was. She was as much, if not more, to blame. If only she'd stood up to him at the start and said what was in her heart, he would have never begun to believe that she didn't want him.

How had he survived?

"Because he's strong," she whispered to the darkness. Strong and used to fighting for everything he'd ever gotten from life. But he'd been unable to fight her inhibitions, unable to fight years of Grandmother Ada's pitiless conditioning.

Why hadn't he ever told her what she was doing to him? And why hadn't she ever asked him what he needed, what *he* wanted in bed? Accustomed to Caleb taking charge, she'd always allowed him to focus on pleasing her. Especially in bed. When had she ever tried to please him?

Never.

Her heart clenched. Her inexperience was no excuse, not when she'd soon realized that Caleb needed something from her that she didn't know how to give. Instead of asking him, she'd buried her head in the sand and pretended everything was okay, using the coping tactic that had allowed her to survive after her mother had abandoned her on Ada's doorstep. However, mere survival was no longer enough. She wanted to *live*.

Pushing aside the blanket, she got up and padded down the wide hallway to the kitchen. The romantic glow of the moonlight streaming through the windows seemed to mock her as she pulled a carton of milk from the fridge. Pouring some into a glass, she replaced the carton and put her cold fingers to her eyelids.

A creaking noise came from the hallway and a second later, Caleb entered the kitchen wearing only a pair of black boxer shorts. "What are you doing up?" His voice was rough, his hair mussed.

"I couldn't sleep." She raised her glass in explanation. "Do you want some?" Caleb stood only a few feet from her and yet miles away. She didn't know if she had the courage to cross the divide.

He merely raised an eyebrow at the offer.

Finishing her drink, she put the glass in the sink and rubbed her hands on the thighs of her flannel pj's. "Did I wake you?" Was she going to pretend that he hadn't left her naked and alone in bed? Continue living her life in a fantasy world? Or was she finally going to say what needed to be said?

"No."

God, he was so beautiful to her and she was so afraid to touch him. Swallowing, she crossed the cool tiles until she was less than an arm's length away. "I guess you have a busy day tomorrow. You should try to sleep." Why couldn't she say what she so desperately wanted to say?

She tried to force the truth out, fighting years of being told that passion and desire were dangerous and destructive. Words bubbled up in her throat but no matter how hard she pushed, fear kept her lips from shaping them into sound.

Something like disappointment flickered in Caleb's eyes but she couldn't be sure in the semidarkness of the room. He simply moved to let her pass, then fell in step behind her. She heard him enter the guest bedroom a few seconds after she'd shut the door to the master bedroom and slumped against it.

More tears burned at the back of her eyes, mute evidence of her frustration and anger. What was wrong with her? Was she so cowardly that she couldn't even take the necessary steps toward saving her marriage? Was she going to settle for this half-life, with her husband thinking she couldn't bear his touch?

So angry with herself that she wanted to scream, she forced herself to remember each moment of the two months she'd spent alone in this house. Every single day she'd come into this bedroom, crawled into this bed and hungered for Caleb. She'd slept on his side of the mattress, worn his old shirts, spent entire nights dreaming of his loving.

Was she willing to go back to that existence? Because she knew without a doubt that her husband wasn't going to return to her bed unless she convinced him she needed him desperately. She'd hurt him too much.

It was the thought of Caleb in such pain that straightened her defeated posture. Taking a deep breath, she tucked her hair behind her ears and opened the door.

Caleb's own door was open and she knew why. Even in his anger, he wanted to be able to hear her if she needed him. It was a good sign, she told herself as she walked in. He was lying on his side facing away, but she knew he heard her come in even though he didn't move. For the first time in their married life, Caleb had turned his back to her.

Fighting the hot rush of fear, she crossed the endless carpet and sat on the other side of the bed. As soon as she touched the mattress she knew she was making a mistake. There was only one way she could reach Caleb—she had to stop protecting herself. She moved to lie beside him, her head nestled in the hollow of his back, one hand on his waist.

"What are you doing here, Vicki?"

She'd never heard him sound that harsh, that unwelcoming. It shot her confidence to pieces but she was here and if she could come this far, she could keep going. "You walked away without letting me explain."

"What's there to explain?"

So much, she thought desperately, that she couldn't find the words for. "I didn't know," she whispered. "I didn't know you thought I didn't want you. I swear, I didn't know." She'd thought *she* was doing something wrong and had tried to control her own reactions so as not to offend him, not realizing she was taking the worst possible action.

Caleb didn't reach out to gather her into his arms as he had so many nights in the past. She ached to be held. But it wasn't easy for a woman who'd spent a lifetime hiding her emotions to lay them out in the open.

"Now you do."

And the next step was hers.

The thing was, Vicki didn't know how to take that next step, didn't know how to fix this broken bridge between them. She'd never confided in him, never once taken the chance of putting her pride, her heart, her deep insecurities on the line.

"You have to help me," she whispered. If she was going to lose her husband, it wouldn't be because she'd been too afraid to chance her heart. "I can't do this without you."

At last, he turned. But he didn't hold her, instead propping himself up on his elbow. "We've had enough lies between us. Just tell me the truth. Why?"

Why did you marry me if you can't stand my touch?

The words he'd spoken in anger earlier whispered around the room, a silent third party to this painful conversation.

"I love your touch," she repeated her own words. But this time when he began to move away, she grabbed his shoulder. "*Don't.* Don't, Caleb."

It was the break in Vicki's voice that halted Caleb. He knew she was fighting tears. No matter how much it hurt him to lie beside her knowing she felt nothing for him when he burned for her, he'd do it if it would stop her from crying. He had no defense against her tears, not when he knew exactly what they cost her.

In the early days of their marriage, she'd once confessed that she didn't cry because as a child, her tears had been the only thing over which she'd had any control. No matter what she'd said or done, her grandmother had never been able to make Vicki break down.

"I'm here," he said. "Don't cry, honey."

"I'm not crying." Her voice was raw. "I just need to say this. I've been trying for so long."

"What?" Giving in to his own need, he drew her into his arms. She came without hesitation, spooning her back to his front. The familiarity of the gesture was bittersweet. Vicki didn't mind his embrace. All those late nights when he'd finally slipped into bed, she'd sleepily scooted nearer so he could tuck her close.

"The way I am in bed…it's not your fault."

What was he supposed to make of that?

She took a deep, halting breath. "Grandmother…"

The abrupt change of topic threw him. "What about her?"

Caleb didn't particularly like Ada Wentworth, even though the old woman had introduced him to Vicki and given her smiling blessing to their union. He'd known that Ada had chosen to overlook his lack of breeding only because of his increasing wealth and connections, but it hadn't mattered. Despite the ten-year gap in their ages, he'd fallen headlong for Vicki.

She put her hand over the arm he had around her waist. "She said— She said that the reason my father left my mother was because my mother was a s-slut. A w-whore who'd spread her legs for any man who asked."

Caleb bit off a sharp curse. "How old were you?" He knew she'd been sent to live with Ada at four years of age, soon after her parents, Danica and Gregory Wentworth, had divorced.

"I can't remember the first time, but I grew up with her voice in my head telling me 'like mother, like daughter.' I guess I must have been very young when she started. There was never a time when I didn't know what Grandmother thought of Mother and what she'd think of me if I ever strayed out of line."

He was rocked by the viciousness of the wounds Vicki had hidden inside herself.

"And she said," Vicki continued before he could speak, "that unless I was the perfect model of a wife, you'd leave me, too. She told me that men don't want their wives to be w-whores. If I wanted to keep you, I had better make sure I *always* acted like a lady, not a slut."

She was killing him. "Vicki—"

"When I was ten, my father married Claire. She's so perfect, sometimes I don't think she's real. It's as if she has ice running in her veins. I've never seen her show any powerful emotion. Grandmother used to tell me, 'Look at Claire and now look at Danica. Men sleep with sluts, but they marry women of breeding.' I believed her."

Caleb wanted to strangle Ada. "I married you," he said, trying to cut through her pain. "I never asked you to be anything other than the woman you were."

"That's just it, Caleb." Haunting sadness laced her tone. "You were so proud to be marrying the woman Grandmother had made me into, the woman I was when we met. So proud of the way I talked and acted. I wanted you to love me so I tried hard to continue to be that woman even though she wasn't really me.

"And all the time, I knew I wasn't giving you what you needed but I didn't understand what it was that I was doing wrong. I kept trying harder and harder but no matter what I did, you kept moving further away from me. Then one day I realized that if I tried any harder to be someone I wasn't, I'd disappear forever."

Stunned, he put both hands on her shoulders and tugged her onto her back with him braced over her. She tried to avoid his gaze but he put a finger on her jaw and applied gentle pressure until her eyes met his. "You don't have to act a certain way to prove yourself to me. The only thing I ever wanted was for you to drop your shields and let me in."

Her eyes widened at his husky words. A hesitant hand rose to touch his cheek and he felt his whiskers scrape her skin. He used to shower and shave before coming to her, wanting to be what he'd *thought* she needed.

"Really?" Doubt continued to throw shadows over her expression.

Understanding, he stroked the hair off her face. "Don't you think I could tell what Ada had tried to do to you? What attracted me to you was your spirit, your refusal to be crushed by her. I was so goddamn proud to have you as my wife. *You,* not the well-bred, elegant doll."

"And I was proud to have you as my husband." Vicki's hand slid to rest on his shoulder. "Proud of what you'd achieved through sheer determination. Did you know I used to brag to the other wives about your successful cases? Sometimes, I'd go sit in the back of the courtroom to watch you work and think, *he's mine.*"

Caleb's whole world changed in that instant. "Vicki," he whispered. No one had ever been proud of him. His family came to him for money but not one of them had ever said, "Well done, Caleb, well done." Not one of them had ever come to watch him defend a case. And not one of them had ever been so proud that they'd praised him to others.

"I'm sorry," she said. "I'm so sorry."

He shook his head. "I'm as much to blame as you. I pushed and pushed like I always do." As a child, belligerence had been the only way he'd been able to make his father, Max, "see" him. As often as not, his stubbornness had sparked Max's temper, but back then Caleb had been desperate enough to value *any* connection with the man. The experience had scarred him, made him emotionally aggressive when dealing with the people who mattered to him, with Vicki.

"And I let you," she added, taking a burden that should never have set on her shoulders. "Every time I tried to speak about it, I'd get so nervous and when you began to soothe me and say we could talk about whatever it was later, I'd agree. But later never came."

Caleb wasn't going to allow her to let him off the hook so easily. "Honey, I knew you wanted to tell me something…I just didn't want to hear it. I thought," he dropped his head and owned up to his colossal blunder, "that you'd tell me you didn't want to be in bed with me. So I tried to change your mind each time." Another assumption, he realized, beginning to see the pattern in his dealings with Vicki.

Her eyes were huge. "What happens next?"

"I want to be married to you, Vicki." Nothing subtle would work now. "Do you want to be married to me?"

The pause was minuscule. "Yes." She took a deep breath. "*Yes.*"

It wasn't the avowal he'd been looking for. But it was better than her earlier statement that they were still separated. "Then giving up is not an option." It had never been for him. And despite Vicki's ambivalence, he didn't think it had ever been for her, either. If it had, she would have taken his key when she'd kicked him out and refused to see him those times he'd come over or invited her to lunch. But she hadn't.

"Caleb…" She put a hesitant hand on his upper arm. "Do you want…? We can try again."

The vulnerability he could see shattered him. He knew that right now, he could ask for anything in bed and she'd try to provide it. But he didn't want his wife giving in to him because she was laboring under a burden of guilt. He wanted them to bridge this distance in the bright light of day.

"All I want is for you to sleep in my arms." He dropped

a soft kiss on her lips. It was one of the hardest things he'd ever done. Part of him—the part that had been deprived for years—whispered that he should take this chance, that it might never come again, that this emotional woman in his arms would be gone when morning arrived, replaced by the cool, elegant lady he barely dared to touch.

Troubled eyes met his. "Caleb, I can…"

"Hush." He moved onto his back, pulling her against his chest. "Sleep. This is enough for tonight." Despite the desperate voices urging him to take what she was trying to offer and not look back, he knew he spoke the truth. His wife was used to keeping her emotions well under control. And yet she'd come to him tonight.

Finally, she'd come to him.

Five

Vicki woke to the sound of Caleb showering. As always, she fantasized about going into the bathroom, stripping off her clothing and joining him in that steamy enclosure. What she'd give to run her hands over his soap-slick skin, to explore his beautiful body as she wished. But as always, she got out of bed and went to put on the coffee instead.

"One day," she muttered under her breath as she set the coffeemaker. "One day *soon*." She'd love to shock Caleb by joining him. He'd never expect that. And he was probably right—she didn't have the kind of sexual confidence it took to approach a man naked and vulnerable, assured that he'd accept, not reject, her silent invitation.

Getting the bread out of the pantry, she was struck by the appearance of her hands—the oval nails polished a pale nude color, the tasteful wedding band that was her only jewelry. It seemed to her that she was exactly like her hand—well polished, boring and without character. Not a woman who did exciting things like surprise her husband in the shower.

The scent of Caleb's woodsy aftershave warned her that he'd entered the kitchen. Without thinking about it, she turned and blurted, "Am I boring, Caleb?"

His eyes widened. "You might be a lot of things, honey, but boring isn't one of them."

"Tell me one thing I've done that's been out of the ordinary." She put the bread on the counter and frowned. "One thing I've done that you never expected me to do."

"You asked me for a divorce." He grabbed a couple of slices of bread and put them in the toaster. "Then you told me to go sleep in the guest bedroom—surprised the hell out of me and not in a good way."

She breathed in the just-showered scent of him and wanted nothing more than to pull him down by that sedate navy tie and plant a shockingly raw good-morning kiss on his lips. Caleb had always looked good in a suit. "Hmm," she said, staring at him as he reached up to get mugs from the upper cupboards. "Caleb?"

He put two mugs on the counter. "Yes?"

"Are we going to ignore last night?" She couldn't bear to pretend anymore. It was as if once she'd ripped open this scar she had to keep pushing at it to see how much it hurt, to check if it had healed any.

He faced her, tall, strong and masculine to the core. When she thought he'd speak, he cupped her face in his hands and kissed her. She melted into him, clutching at his waist to keep herself upright. Usually Caleb let her control their kisses, but today he was kissing the thoughts right out of her head.

When they came up for air, his eyes were filled with a thousand emotions. "What do you think?"

Barely able to breathe, she pointed to the toaster. "Your toast's ready."

For some reason, that made him smile. "I made you a piece, too." He buttered the toast and put it to her lips. "You're eating for two now, Mrs. Callaghan."

The unbearably *Caleb* statement, care wrapped in action, made her smile. And that was how she sent her husband off to work. For the first time in a long while, they laughed as they kissed each other goodbye, looking forward to the night to come.

Once Caleb had left, Vicki went through some catalogues for the university and a nearby technical college. It had come as a rude shock during the separation to realize that without Caleb, she was a woman who did nothing useful, nothing that made her proud. With no client dinners to organize or cocktail parties to attend, no suits to be dry-cleaned, no husband to mess up the pristine house, she'd been slapped with the fact that part of her anger at Caleb came from her own uninspiring existence.

Her husband was a dynamo in the legal world, respected by colleagues and competitors alike. And what was she? A *finishing school*-educated woman of twenty-four. She kept up with Caleb by reading business journals voraciously so she could discuss things he was interested in. But how long would that sustain them? How long until it became clear to him that she had nothing original to contribute to their lives?

But her urge to do more wasn't all about pleasing Caleb. It was about her. Caleb and the baby were her life, her everything. Was that healthy? Would she wake up one day to find her child grown and Caleb buried in work, leaving her alone and adrift? Would she become like her grandmother, convincing herself that jewels and parties could fill the void where her dreams and goals, her self-respect, should have resided?

And what if their marriage failed despite everything? She didn't have a shred of doubt that Caleb would support her and their child, but she wanted to be able to take care of herself, wanted to be more than she was right now. It would have been one thing if she'd chosen to be a home-maker because it was right for her, but she hadn't. She'd just drifted into it because it was what Caleb seemed to want.

It was time to make her own choices.

But no matter how much she tried to convince herself that study was a good idea, she couldn't get past her need to *do* something. Another two or three years in academic limbo seemed like a life sentence after the years she'd already lost. But what could she do? What was she quali-fied for?

Nothing.

Even more frustrated than when she'd started, she put away the catalogues and spent the rest of the day pulling non-existent weeds from the back garden. The portable phone beside her rang mid-afternoon. It was her mother.

"Did you get my card? I'll be flying into Auckland sometime in the next couple of weeks. Coffee?" Danica asked in that voice that had acquired a slight Mediterra-nean accent over the years.

Vicki agreed, aware that it was more than likely Danica would forget to keep the date. Her mother's haphazard visits were something Vicki had gotten used to. At least that was what she told herself. "Give me a call when you get in."

Hanging up after a quick goodbye, she started pulling weeds with too much force, sending dirt flying every-where. It took her ten minutes to calm down enough to realize she'd pulled out most of the dark purple and yellow pansies she loved. How did her mother always manage to agitate her so much?

Forcing herself to think through the furious buzz of emotion, Vicki apologized to the plants, replanted the ones that weren't too bedraggled and began to reorganize a border of stones around the garden. After a while, the repetitive physical activity numbed her emotions enough that she felt marginally better, though she knew it was a delaying tactic against not only dealing with her future, but also her chaotic feelings toward Danica.

She was picking up a big stone to reposition it for the seventy-sixth time when Caleb walked around the side of the house. He'd taken the stone from her before she could say a word of welcome. "Where?" he asked, face grim.

She pointed to the right spot. "You look like you saw a ghost."

He set down the stone and straightened. "I saw my *pregnant* wife threatening to kill herself hauling stones that didn't need to be moved." He was scowling, clearly not amused.

She rolled her eyes. "I was fine." Then she grinned. "You're home in time for dinner."

"I was hoping you'd notice." He rubbed a smudge of dirt off her nose. "Have you been rolling around in the mud again?"

Laughing, she took off a glove and pushed at him. "Change. Then come help me in the kitchen." For a second, their camaraderie was like when they'd first married. He'd come home countless times to tease her that she looked like a laborer's assistant with her broken nails and paint-splattered overalls. Then he'd lift her up in his arms and swing her around, both of them laughing with happiness simply because they were together.

Caleb's grin faded as she stared at him. "What do you see?" he asked.

"Us. Before we lost each other." The words came from somewhere deep in her soul where they'd been trapped for what seemed like forever. Under her hand, his heart beat strong and loud, but she wondered if it still beat for her as passionately as it once had.

"We're not done yet," he said. "Not by a long shot." The stubborn set of his jaw was as familiar to her as her own face, and welcome beyond measure. "You have dirt in your hair." He picked at the strands by her temple.

"I need to shower," she whispered, her voice husky.

For a moment, she thought he heard what she was trying to say, heard the woman in her attempting to come out of hiding, but then he dropped his hand and the moment was gone. "I'll let you clean up and meet you in the kitchen."

She tried not to let her disappointment show. "Okay."

They were just sitting down to dinner at the kitchen table when the phone rang. Caleb picked up the extension on the wall to answer it as she went to grab a forgotten bottle of salad dressing.

"Yes, I'm listening."

Her head jerked up at the tone of his voice. Gone was all the humor, sensuality, laughter. Tightly controlled, he sounded almost emotionless and there were only a few people who made him sound that way. "Your family? Lara?" she mouthed.

He gave a sharp nod. "How much?"

Vicki narrowed her eyes, in no doubt as to why Lara had called. It was the same reason why any of his family ever called. She was acquainted with all three members—Caleb had never hidden his roots. Before they'd married, he'd taken her to the run-down neighborhood where he'd grown up and introduced her to his family and friends.

She knew that Max was a sculptor and Caleb's mother, Carmen, a poet. Unfortunately, neither had achieved professional success. To Victoria, Max and Carmen had always seemed sanctimonious in their assertions that they were sacrificing for their art. What they'd sacrificed was their children's welfare. Caleb rarely talked about his growing-up years, but from what he had let slip, she'd guessed that he'd sometimes gone hungry.

Unlike Caleb, his sister, Lara, hadn't left the family fold. A struggling singer with two kids by two different men, she'd never wavered from her belief that her parents' way—poverty and suffering as the only path to creative genius—was the right way.

"What did she want?" Vicki asked when Caleb hung up the phone and came to stand beside her.

He sighed, staring blindly into space. "What she always wants. Money. Since I sold out to the capitalist regime, the least I can do is help her out now and then." His tone was flat, as if the call had drained all emotion from him.

Vicki recognized the familiar refrain. She'd heard it enough times from Lara's own mouth. Previously, Vicki had remained silent, reasoning that she had no business interfering with Caleb and his family. Now, seeing the pain revealed by her husband's bowed head, she decided it was very much her business.

Turning slightly, she pushed at his chest until he looked at her. "Why do you let them treat you this way?" Instinct told her there was something fundamental she didn't know. The political rhetoric the Callaghans spewed simply couldn't explain the antipathy Vicki sometimes felt emanating from them toward Caleb. What wasn't he telling her?

She knew she didn't yet have the right to push for that information. They'd barely started talking about repairing the fissures in their marriage. Until those wounds had healed, she had to tread softly. But it didn't mean she had to remain silent.

He shrugged. "They're my family."

"No," she said. "They abandoned you when you dared to be different." She knew he'd left home at sixteen and scraped by on his own, working multiple jobs while going to school. His parents had kicked him out when he'd dared argue with them about what he wanted from life. "They've never been there for you."

A bleak look appeared in his eyes. "They're all I've got."

She shook her head, furious at them for always causing him such pain. "*We're* your family, Caleb. Me and our baby."

"But you might be divorcing me." It wasn't a challenge but a reminder of their precarious situation. Before he could blink it away, she glimpsed an incredible anguish that had nothing to do with Lara or his parents and everything to do with her.

A crushing knot formed in her heart. God, but the man was proud. Proud and stubborn. Not once in those two months of separation had he ever hinted at the depth of his pain at the way she'd asked him to leave. Then again, neither had she ever told him how badly he'd hurt her when he'd taken Miranda to his bed. They were both too good at keeping their emotional secrets.

But that, she thought with a new spurt of determination, was in the past. It was the future that was important—a future built on trust, shared burdens and hope. Maybe asking for a separation had been the only way she'd known to get him to pay attention to their marriage, to *her,* but they'd gone beyond that now.

This was it. Time for action. Despite her fear that she'd do the wrong thing and their truce would go bad all over again, she nonetheless shook her head. "No. I'm not. I told you I want to be married to you. You're my husband, my family. *I don't have anyone else, either.*"

He hauled her into a tight hug, saying with his body what he couldn't say in words. For so long, he'd spoken with his body but she hadn't been listening, hadn't known how to listen, but now she intended to hear every single whisper.

"It's Lara's kids I worry about. She can look after herself but what about them?"

Vicki had always been swayed by the same thought. "How about a trust fund? For education and anything else the kids might need. Your family doesn't get to treat you like an open checkbook anymore." It wasn't the money that made her mad, but the way they acted as if it was Caleb's duty to support them while putting up with their ingratitude.

She'd never been able to understand why her tough, powerful husband let them get away with it. She knew that taking care of Lara's children wouldn't even scratch at the surface of Caleb's problems with his family, or tell her anything of the reasons behind the way they treated him. But it was a start.

Caleb was silent for a moment. "If we were the trustees, we could ensure the money was used how it was meant to be."

Neither of them had to mention their fears that Lara might have succumbed to drugs. But, so far, she'd never harmed her kids, apparently being a devoted mother.

"Yes," Vicki agreed, then decided to say something that had been bubbling up inside of her for quite some time. "Don't you dare let them make you feel bad because you dreamed higher than they have the capacity to imagine. Be proud." The Callaghans' motivations made no difference to her. In her book, nothing could excuse the neglect and pain Caleb had suffered because of them.

His chin dropped to rest on top of her head. "They'll always be in my life."

"And I'll never try to push them out. We both have relations we have to deal with though we'd rather not. But they have to learn to treat you with the proper respect." She refused to back off on this. Too many times in their marriage, she'd stayed silent and it had torn them apart. However, that particular dam had broken forever when she'd walked into Caleb's room and bared her soul. "Next time one of them calls, I'll take it. This is the last chance they'll ever have to hurt you."

Caleb was astounded by the cold fury he could hear in her voice. Vicki had always been so gentle, so non-confrontational. But beyond his surprise was the glow of hope. She was right. He was holding his real family in his arms. Maybe their marriage was rocky but they'd made a promise to see it through. The lack of ambivalence in Vicki's comments gave him back the sense of stability he'd lost the moment she'd demanded a divorce.

"I want to ask you something," he said, reminded of it by his thoughts of the cool, non-combative woman he'd married. A woman in whom he'd seen embers of passion— embers that their marriage had stifled instead of nurtured.

"What?" Vibrant life in that single word.

A little of his guilt receded. "What did your grandmother tell you when she invited me to that dinner party where she introduced us?" Lately, he'd begun to wonder if Ada had lied to get Vicki to trust him enough to let him court her. How else could he explain her faith in him from the very start? Especially when his no-holds-barred personality must have been immediately obvious.

Laughing, she tipped her head back to meet his gaze. "She said she'd found the perfect man for me. He'd keep me in line because I'd need a strong hand to ensure I didn't turn out like my mother. Oh, and he'd make sure I was taken care of."

He winced, his theory in ruins. That was hardly likely to get a woman to trust a man. "Did she force you—"

"I fell for you about ten seconds after you started talking to me. She saw a man who'd use his strength to crush. I saw someone who'd use it to protect." She smiled. "You had so much energy, so much heart that you made me feel truly alive for the first time. I couldn't bear to return to the life I had before I met you."

Despite his decision to be honest, Caleb couldn't bring himself to ask the question that continued to haunt him. What about now? Did the woman she'd become trust him as that vulnerable girl had? Or had that love crumbled after years of being trapped in a marriage that made her desperately unhappy?

Instead of asking questions that might destroy him, he joked, "I'm glad because once I saw you, that was it."

"Good." Her laughter was a gift. After hugging him tightly once more, she pulled away. "Come on, let's eat. I'm starving—our baby is a hungry little thing."

"What does it feel like?" he asked, curious.

"The baby? I think I can feel her moving but it's probably all in my mind. According to the baby books, it's too early."

"Her?" That quickly, their baby became real, a little person with hopes and dreams, and a heart that he could bruise with a careless word.

Vicki gave him a sheepish smile. "I just started thinking of it as a girl. Would you prefer a girl or a boy?"

"I don't mind," he replied truthfully. "I only want it to be healthy."

"Me, too." Her face became solemn. "It's scary thinking about a child who's going to rely on me for everything."

"On us." He tucked a strand of her hair behind her ear and nudged her into a seat. "But yeah, it's not like either of us has a good example to follow. Are these baby books for dads as well?" Books he understood—they taught you things. Maybe they could teach him how to be a good father, a concept that caused raw panic inside of him whenever he dared think about it. Like now.

Her smile was huge. "Yes. I'll give you a good one."

Sitting down, he nodded. "So," he said, deciding that that was about as much baby talk as he could handle for one night, "you get any interesting phone calls today?" It was meant to be a lighthearted comment but her expression grew pensive.

"Mother confirmed her plans to visit."

He paused, trying to catch the emotions passing over her face like storm clouds. "What else did she say?"

Vicki shrugged and made a face. "Nothing much—you know her. Do you want some more salad?"

He let her change the subject, having learned that she didn't like discussing her mother. Danica contacted Vicki once or twice every year and inevitably left behind a mess. After her last visit, Vicki had locked herself in her study and sobbed as though her heart was broken. Although he'd tried to talk to her about it, she'd pretended nothing was wrong. It frustrated him but her emotional armor on this topic was so tough, he'd never made much of a dent in it.

Figuring they had bigger problems to solve, he didn't press the issue this time. But part of him worried about exactly what it was that she was so scared to face…and what those buried truths were doing to her already-bruised psyche.

They were hyper-aware of each other as they got ready for bed that night. Vicki felt like a virgin again, flustered and lost, with no idea what to do. In the end she washed up and waited until Caleb went into the bathroom to brush his teeth before slipping into her pj's. They were hardly the sexiest of garments, but she wasn't sure she could live up to the promise implied by slinky lingerie.

Sliding under the thick blanket, she turned off all the lights except the one on Caleb's side of the bed. The door to the bathroom opened a second later and Caleb walked back in.

"Sweetheart, that blanket has to go."

Surprised out of her mini panic, she sat straight up. "What?"

He was already pulling it off. "We'll roast to death."

She clutched at her end. "Caleb! It's cold. I need it."

His eyes met hers, the clear hazel almost silver in the muted light of the room. "You needed it. *We* won't."

Heart somewhere in her throat, she released her grip on the blanket. Caleb bunched it up in his hands and walked out. A couple of minutes later, he returned with a much thinner one. Getting in beside her, he flipped it open over them and switched off the light. Then he turned to take her in his arms. She felt his body heat seep into her bones, the most intimate of caresses. He wore only his boxers and the hairs of his bare arm tantalized the skin of her abdomen where the top of her pj's had ridden up.

"Caleb?"

"Yes?"

"I'm scared."

Vicki's confession ripped the heart right out of him. Because the truth was, he was terrified. Part of him still couldn't accept that she wanted him. It was hard to believe the words she said when he'd spent years listening to her body and hearing the opposite.

"There's nothing to be scared about. All you have to do is let your body tell the truth." What he didn't want to face was the prospect that he'd hear the same unwelcoming message.

He didn't think he had it in him to go back to the way things had been before Vicki had shaken up their world. Now that he'd glimpsed the fire within her, he wanted to plunge his hand into the flames and burn in the heat of her passion.

Turning in his arms, Vicki tipped her head up. He could barely see the outline of her face. "I want you so much, Caleb. Please don't give up on me."

"I don't think I have it in me to give up on you." Sliding the hand on her hip up into her hair, he moved his body slightly over hers and placed a kiss on her lips.

Fire and spice, ecstasy and exquisite pleasure, her kiss was everything he could have asked for. She said everything with her lips, her tongue, her breathless gasps. But this time he couldn't get past the fact that her arms remained by her sides.

Breaking the kiss, his initial reaction was to move away, to save himself another knife in the heart.

You have to help me.

Her plea from the night before filled his mind as he reached down, lifted one arm and put it over his shoulder. She gave a soft "Ohh," and did the same with her other. "Sorry," she whispered against his lips. "I forget everything when you kiss me."

Caleb thought a man could hear worse things in bed. Leaning down, he kissed her again but let her take the lead. Every particle of his being was concentrated on her body, on the way she moved, on the slightest pressure of her fingertips.

"This isn't working," she said, pulling away from the kiss. "You're so tense I can feel your muscles vibrating and I'm even worse."

It was in his nature to argue but he knew she was right. Swearing under his breath, he rolled onto his back. Both of them stared at the ceiling. Now what?

"P-perhaps we should talk first before we rush into... We never talked, Caleb." The words were hesitant, but in her tone he heard a thread of strength that told him that maybe, just maybe, she was ready to face all that he needed from her. Not only from her body but from her soul.

The question was, would she be willing to give it to him? He knew he wasn't an easy man to live with, to love. He was too demanding, too protective and, on occasion, downright autocratic.

The woman he'd married five years ago had captured his heart with her shy intensity, but she hadn't had the grit to stand up to him. Instead of fighting when he'd become too domineering, she'd withdrawn. But now, his Vicki was coming out of hiding. They could explore what that might mean for their marriage.

"Why didn't you touch me in bed?" he asked. "I can understand how uncertain Ada must have made you but I never stopped you from doing that. I *asked* you to."

She took in a quick breath but didn't retreat. "I was afraid of doing something wrong. You can't imagine how terrified I was that I'd make a mistake and disgust you. You were so important to me and all I had for guidance was what Grandmother had taught me and what I'd seen between Claire and my father—separate bedrooms and separate lives."

He could hear the deep emotion in her voice and it took everything he had not to take her back into his arms, to soothe her pain. The wounds between them couldn't be so easily solved—they had to confront the mess they'd created in this bed and it seemed fitting that the truth was coming out in the darkness, in the same heavy silence that had hidden their past mistakes.

"I was too shy to bring up the topic with my friends— it's such a private thing. Of course I watched TV and read magazines but Grandmother had beaten it into me that I was…flawed goods. I couldn't be anything less than perfect because *any* mistake might lead to a total loss of control. And then I'd be rejected and end up like my mother—mistress to a man married to another woman. It was the perfect threat. I wanted a husband, a family."

Caleb could hear echoes of the lost girl she'd been, the teenager with no one but a bitter, angry woman to teach her. He wished he could go back in time and kiss away Vicki's pain but all he could do was listen.

She put one hand on his shoulder, hesitant, searching. "So I tried to do as she said. But she didn't tell me how far I could go with my husband, didn't tell me what it was that I couldn't do. I didn't know the rules so I froze. And after a while, you stopped trying to teach me."

He knew she was right. He'd arrogantly expected her to follow his lead, never asking if that was what she wanted, never stopping to listen to her unspoken needs. But some mistakes could be rectified. "Tell me what would make it easier for you."

Her fingers stilled. Turning over at last, he propped himself over her. "Don't stop speaking to me now," he said, not sure he could cope if he had to do this over again. His male ego was already bruised and battered.

"It's so hard to say." Her voice was a whisper. "The only thing I need is your patience."

"Slow, honey? Is that what you want?"

Her hands moved between them to press softly against his chest. "Yes."

He traced patterns across the delicate skin of her neck, aching for her. "Do you really want me, Vicki?"

He needed the answer to that blunt question, even if the wrong answer could wound him beyond repair. As he finished speaking, he shifted subtly, letting her feel his arousal against her thigh. He wanted her, had always wanted her. No other woman could do this to him.

She gasped. *"Caleb."* Her skin flushed hot against his fingertips and she put both hands on his shoulders. He thought for a second that she was going to push him away and his heart plummeted. Then her fingers curved and she tugged him closer. "How can you always do this to me? We've been together for five years."

"Do what to you?" Fascinated by the way her body was *melting* to accommodate his, he could hardly speak.

Another silence, but this time it was filled with the heat of their hunger. "Needy, hot…starving for you."

Six

Caleb's breath rushed out of him. Unable to form words, he used touch to tell her how he felt. Sliding his hand down, he spread his fingers over her belly, indulging himself as he'd wanted to do since forever. Soon, this barely curved plane would round and he'd explore that change day by sweet day without worrying that his embrace was unwelcome or unwanted.

Something hot and beautiful sparked inside his heart at the thought of the tiny life hidden inside his wife's body. A life that had been so determined to be born it had circumvented all their precautions. He was already proud of their kid's stubbornness.

"It feels like the first time," Vicki whispered.

He leaned down. "For both of us." Their mouths met. Sweet temptation.

That was what she'd always tasted like. The sweetest,

most luscious of temptations. Except now, there was an edge to the taste of her, a spicy bite. His body grew heavy with need, captivated by this woman who was half stranger and so sexy, he thought he might die from the intensity of the desire riding him.

Then her hands began moving hesitantly down his chest, caressing him through the hair there. After so many years of hunger, he could scarcely bear the almost painful pleasure. When she began to circle her fingers around his nipples, his breath grew jagged, the sound harsh in the intimate silence.

"Caleb?" Breaking the kiss, she stilled.

"Don't stop, Vicki. I've waited years for your touch." He let her see his need, let her see the things he'd hidden from her, too damn proud to make himself vulnerable.

"Will you…will you tell me if I do something that I shouldn't?"

Her courage amazed him. "I swear to you I will never be turned off by anything you do in this bed."

Her body shuddered. "It almost killed me not to…" Her fingers began to move again, stroking and petting and learning. "So many times I wanted to tell you but then I'd think that ladies weren't supposed to discuss sex, that it would turn you from me. How could I have been so stupid?"

"Hush." He kissed her. "You were worried and inexperienced, and I'm not the easiest of men to talk to. Forget the past—from now on it's you and me in this bed, no lies, no regrets."

"No regrets." Those slender fingers slid down to caress his abdomen, his waist, his back.

Trying to find the strength to let her explore him as she needed to do, he reclaimed her lips. And drowned in the feel of her, in the exquisite lushness of the sensuality she'd released from bondage. Her kiss promised the same ecstasy it always had. But this time his body thrummed with the knowledge that the promise would be fulfilled if only he was patient.

Delicate hands stroked his back before returning to his chest. He wanted to demand a more intimate touch, something he'd never asked of her, but even enslaved by passion, he knew she had to make that decision on her own. He was utterly at her mercy. She could heal him or break him.

Her hand brushed past his navel.

"Lower," he grit out, unable to stay silent. "Sorry."

She kissed his jaw. "No. I want you to tell me. I need you to."

He was having trouble thinking with her hand where it was. Then one of her fingers plucked at the waistband of his boxers and he groaned, "Lower, honey." His voice was so rough, he barely understood himself.

"Like this?"

Shudders racked him as her fingers slipped under the waistband to carefully grasp his erection. Burying his face in her neck, he tried to breathe as she began to stroke him slow and hard. He fisted the sheets in his hands, refusing to bruise her by crushing her skin in a grip gone feral.

Under his chest, her breasts were soft, her nipples beautifully pebbled even through her pajama top, but he was too blinded by unexpected pleasure to pay homage to them. Shocked by the fury of the fire arcing through him, he had no choice but to surrender. And in that moment, Caleb did something he hadn't done in five years of marriage. He lost control.

The climax hit him hard and fast, a knockout punch that left him a heavy weight on her, drained, heart racing at a thousand miles an hour. "I'm sorry," he rasped when he could speak.

To his surprise, she kissed his neck and said, "Do you really want me that much?" Her free hand lifted to brush sweat-damp hair off his forehead.

"I've always wanted you." The single reason he'd never before surrendered so completely was because the wanting had seemed one-sided. That painful knowledge had always blunted his physical pleasure. He'd gone to her bed but part of him had stayed separate, trying to protect himself from the hurt he knew would come.

"I want to please you again," she whispered, nuzzling his throat. "I want to feel you wanting me. I need to know that you like it when I...when I let go." She swallowed and he felt the movement. "I can't quite convince myself that it's okay to be like this with you."

He sucked in a breath when he realized she was still holding him intimately. "Sweetheart, believe me, I'd love to oblige you but I'm thirty-four years old. I don't recover quite so fast anymore."

Her hand began to stroke and squeeze, while her lips trailed along the edge of his jaw. "Please, Caleb?"

He'd taught his body to be satisfied with barely a taste when he wanted to gorge. About to tell her it would take time no matter how much he wanted to indulge her, he felt his body roar to life. She began placing suckling kisses on his neck as her free hand played over his chest.

"I want to give you..." he began.

Her hand tightened a fraction, sending shock waves over his body. "You've given me enough pleasure for two lifetimes. I owe you. Let me, Caleb, honey. Let me." The last was a sensual plea.

He didn't stand a chance.

* * *

When he woke the next morning, Vicki was gone from the bed but he could hear her singing in the kitchen. Grinning, he got up, feeling like a teenager. They hadn't made love last night but he wasn't complaining. It would come.

If he was patient.

Caleb had never been much good at patience but damn if he wasn't going to win a gold medal in it this time around. He was still grinning as he ducked into the shower. Fifteen minutes later, he finished putting on his tie and walked into the kitchen.

Vicki was at the stove, flipping pancakes. He loved pancakes but she usually only made them on weekends. Coming up behind her, he slipped his arms around her waist and kissed her neck. "Good morning."

She went bright red as she mumbled "Good morning." Turning off the stove, she put the pancakes on a plate.

He knew that part of her had to be worried about what they'd done last night, whether she'd acted the right way or not. Knowing that something was okay, and accepting it were two different things. "I'm looking forward to being patient tonight."

"Caleb Callaghan!" Whirling around in his arms, she met his laughing gaze. "Don't you tease me about this."

"Why not?"

"Because I made you pancakes."

Unable to resist, he kissed her. Her hands wrapped around his waist. They were still a little hesitant but they were there. And her mouth...her mouth was pure temptation. He kissed her with every ounce of passion in him.

When they parted, her lips were swollen, her eyes wide. He never wanted to let her go. She was his wife, the only one he'd ever wanted. If they could get past this, they could get past everything else. "We'll be okay."

"Caleb, this isn't the only problem we had. It might even have been the least of them. I've always wanted you. I just didn't know how to show it."

He was startled by the echo of his thoughts. "But if we can talk about this after so long, we can talk about anything."

"Can we?" Clouds moved over the sunshine of her face. "You're not exactly open. After all this time, I barely know you. I feel like you're only willing to share the *easy* parts of yourself. The rest, you keep locked up tight."

He rested his forehead against hers, rocked by how well she understood him. "I'll fight for you, Vicki. So, fight for me." It was an invitation with terrifying implications. What if she discovered the shame he'd spent a lifetime trying to erase?

Caleb's mood of tentative hope didn't last. An hour after he walked into the office, all hell broke loose with the Donner deal.

Callaghan & Associates was representing the Donner family in the sale of their multi-million-dollar shipping concern to Bentley Corporation. The deal was almost done, the financial negotiations finalized, the legal paperwork drafted. The contract was to be signed today.

"Kent, I don't think I heard you right." Caleb stared at his most competent associate. "I thought you said Abe Donner changed his mind." Abe was the patriarch of the clan, the one who'd founded their business empire. He was eighty-six and the best tactician Caleb had ever seen, but unfortunately, he had an emotional attachment to the shipping part of the family's interests.

Kent winced. "He just sent through a fax. Here." He shoved the fax at Caleb as if getting rid of a bomb.

Caleb read the three-line letter and dropped his head in his hands. He didn't need this right now. He wished Abe Donner to perdition and back and then started thinking about the next steps.

As attorneys for the family, they would, of course, do as the Donners wanted. The problem was, the Donners were split—Abe on one side and the rest of the family on the other. Abe controlled fifty percent of the shares, so without him, Bentley wasn't interested.

"If they don't sign today, Bentley will back out. There's a good chance they'll start negotiations to buy Snow-Hinkerman Lines instead of Donner," Kent said, as if Caleb didn't know.

"And if Bentley backs out, Donner Shipping is going to go down," Caleb muttered. "It's already leeching money from all their other businesses."

"What do we do now?" Kent's face said he knew the answer but didn't want to be the one to say it.

"We advise the family."

Their hastily drafted fax to the other shareholders was like throwing a grenade into a busy street. The shrapnel went every which way and Caleb spent his day trying to referee between the two camps while keeping an already edgy Bentley from throwing in the towel.

Finally, at around one in the morning, Abe conceded defeat to his children and grandchildren and signed on the dotted line. Caleb knew it had been the only viable option given the state of the shipping operations, but he felt for the old man. He'd hate it if someone tried to take Callaghan & Associates from him.

Tired and hungry after having missed both lunch and

dinner, his mind on the files he'd have to catch up on tomorrow, he parked the car in the driveway of the villa, then started to walk up the path. He hadn't gone more than a few feet when the front door opened to reveal Vicki. Dressed in one of his old rugby jerseys, she looked good enough to eat, but he wasn't happy to see her there. "What are you doing up?"

Vicki couldn't miss the lines of tiredness on his face and tried to tell herself to be patient. "Waiting for you." She closed the door behind him and headed to the bedroom, excruciatingly aware of his presence at her back.

"You're pregnant. You need your sleep." He began to undress the second they reached the room.

Getting into bed, she let him get rid of his shoes, belt, jacket and tie before she spoke again. "You're doing it all over again." Her eye fell on the book on the bedside table, the book she'd planned to share with him tonight.

"What?" He shoved his hand through his hair, clearly distracted.

In the past, she'd always left him alone when he got like this, reasoning that the matters on his mind must be very important. That was before she'd realized that nothing was as important as their marriage. "What got us into trouble the first time."

He began to unbutton his shirt. "Christ, Vicki. All I want to do is catch a few hours' sleep and you're trying to start a fight?"

She clenched her fists. "I'm trying to make sure we don't make the same mistakes twice. Don't treat me like I'm not worth listening to!"

"What?" He turned, six feet two inches of male annoyance and rippling muscle under his unbuttoned shirt. "I work late one night and you give me the third degree? This is my job! You know some of the deals have us working day and night for weeks on end. I'm sorry I didn't call but things got a little crazy."

What Vicki heard was that he hadn't even thought about her once work had intervened. It was a painful truth but one she was through avoiding. Caleb's passion was his firm and she couldn't live with that anymore. "Listen to yourself!" Throwing aside the blanket, she knelt on the sheets, her stomach hurting from the tension coiled up inside. "I don't think a man who's gone for weeks on end qualifies as a husband."

He swore under his breath and jerked off his shirt, throwing it to the side. "What do you want me to do? Quit?"

"No. I just want you to think!" Trying to calm herself down, she took a deep breath. The scent of his aftershave shocked her hormones to life, reminding her of the pleasures of the night before, but she couldn't let herself be distracted from this conversation. It was too important. "If you're like this now, how will you make time to be a father? Or will I have to be both mother and father?"

"You've got the time," he shot back. "Or would that get in the way of your lunches with friends?"

She gasped and threw a pillow at him. "Get out!"

"The hell I will! This is my bedroom."

"Fine!" She got off the bed and stalked to the door. "I'll leave."

"*Vicki,*" he growled.

She was too angry to care. Pulling open the door, she headed to the spare bedroom. She felt him behind her and then his arm wrapped around her waist. "Don't be melodramatic," he said, his tone arrogant enough to make her want to scream. "Let's go to bed. We'll talk about it later."

How many times had they said that in their marriage? Frustrated by his unwillingness to even attempt to see things from her perspective, she wrenched herself away. "I want to be alone." Walking into the spare bedroom, she lay down on the bed, facing the wall.

Of course he followed, laying down beside her stiff form. She heard him sigh. "I'm sorry about the lunch crack."

She shrugged, aware that the reason it had hurt so much was because he was right. It was why she'd started looking at those brochures for further education. She did *nothing* while he worked all day. "I don't want to be that woman." The words broke out of her. "It makes me so angry that you see me that way."

"I'm sorry, honey. I really am."

"Yes well, it's true, isn't it? What else am I possibly qualified for? Nothing."

"Come on, Vicki…"

"Forget it, Caleb." She wasn't ready to talk to him about this. Why had she even brought up the subject? "Just stop pushing and let me think."

The body wrapped around hers filled with tension. "So you can talk yourself into something else as equally idiotic as our separation?"

Her simmering temper ignited. "You think me wanting to work outside the home is idiotic?"

"That's not what I said."

"It sure sounded like it. Poor, stupid Vicki. Maybe if you'd supported my needs instead of trying to make me be what you wanted, I wouldn't have had to ask for a separation."

"Now it's all my fault."

Not feeling particularly rational, she said, "Yes."

"Jesus." The arm around her refused to move but she felt his anger. "I'm too exhausted to do this right now."

"Fine."

She felt him fall asleep minutes later, while she lay awake for what seemed like hours, temper, frustration and angry jealously churning in her gut. The truth was a flood-light shining into her eyes. Her husband might have slept with Miranda—might still be sleeping with her—but it was the firm that was his true mistress.

How could Vicki fight that?

Seven

The next morning, Vicki made Caleb some coffee and passed him his toast, munching on a piece of bread as she worked. She wasn't feeling particularly wifely but it had seemed petty to make breakfast for herself and ignore him, notwithstanding the tension that thrummed between them like a high-voltage wire.

Caleb ate quickly and stood. Picking up his coat, he headed out but stopped before he got to the front door. "I better get an early start—I had to let a lot of things slide yesterday."

Not happy at the reminder that the firm had a grip on him stronger than any woman's, she forced herself to say, "Have a good day," as she walked him to the door. Still feeling bruised from their altercation, she was finding it very hard to act as though everything was fine.

He paused with his hand on the doorknob. "I'm not

ignoring what you said last night. I'll be home for dinner but I might have to go back to the office afterward." His eyes met hers. "I can't change the habits of a lifetime overnight."

Her heart warmed. At least he was willing to try to see things from her point of view. She didn't mind if he worked late sometimes, but the problem with Caleb was that he was so driven that *sometimes* could easily turn into *always*. She'd learned that the hard way. "Think of it as practice for being home at bath time and bedtime." If he was willing to try, so was she.

The strain on his face lessened at the acceptance in her voice. "Do you want to go out for dinner?"

She shook her head. "I'd rather spend some quiet time alone. You?"

"Home. I'll aim to arrive around six."

"I'll be waiting."

After he left, Vicki quickly tidied up the house, haunted by the same issue that had so angered her the night before. She still had no idea what she could do for self-improvement. It depressed her how unqualified she was to be anything other than a society wife.

She knew how to mingle, how to be the perfect hostess, how to make people laugh and feel good about themselves, how to create contacts for Caleb and ensure the right people met at dinners or parties—she even knew how to soothe the worst of tempers without making a big deal of it. What job did that qualify her for?

The harsh jangle of the phone interrupted her pity party sometime around mid-morning. She picked it up, surprised to find Caleb on the other end.

"I've set up an appointment for you to talk to someone," he said, sounding harassed. "She'll come by the house at eleven."

"Who?"

"Her name's Helen Smith. I've got to go, sweetheart. One of our major client's sons got picked up for underage drinking. Imbecile. If he wanted to drink, why didn't he ask his father? The man has a wine cellar the size of Texas."

"I didn't know you handled things like that."

"We don't, except as a courtesy to our commercial clients. Everyone else is tied up today so I have to make the court appearance on junior's behalf in twenty minutes."

He hung up without further goodbyes. Surprised and mystified, she saw that she had half an hour before her guest's arrival. Deciding her jeans and pale pink shirt would do, she set about preparing a fresh pot of coffee and some quick biscuits. She was pulling them out of the oven when the doorbell rang.

She opened it to find a woman of around Caleb's age on the doorstep. Dressed in jeans and a navy sweatshirt, she had long auburn hair pulled into a ponytail.

"Ms. Smith?" Vicki held out her hand.

The other woman shook it. "Just Helen. You must be Victoria."

"Please come in."

In the living room, Vicki served coffee and biscuits before saying, "I'm sorry, but my husband didn't tell me much…"

Helen nodded. "He sounded very busy when he called. I'll explain. I met Caleb a year ago when I approached Callaghan & Associates for free legal representation in a messy case involving one of my clients."

Vicki knew that taking on pro bono work was an accepted part of Caleb's practice. He said it kept everyone honest. "I see."

"Kent Jacobs handled the case, but I believe your husband oversaw it." Helen put down her cup and loosely linked her hands together on her knees.

"I'm afraid I still don't see where this is going."

"I'm involved with several charities," Helen explained.

Vicki's heart sank. Was this what Caleb thought she should be doing—sitting on some charity board giving away his money?

"We have a position up for grabs. To be honest the pay sucks, but it is a paid *job.*"

Her attention snapped back to the redhead.

"We're looking for a dedicated fund-raiser for all the charities under an umbrella organization called Heart, someone whose sole focus will be to continuously raise money for us."

Vicki nearly stopped breathing as she recalled her own list of accomplishments.

She knew how to mingle, how to be the perfect hostess, how to make people laugh and feel good about themselves, how to create contacts and ensure the right people met, and how to soothe the worst of tempers without making a big deal of it.

Hope had scarcely started to blossom when she noticed the look on Helen's face. "What is it?"

"I'm going to be honest." The woman's expression was professional. "I'm here as a courtesy because of the help Callaghan & Associates gave us. This job is flexible but it's full time." She frowned, then seemed to opt for brutal truth. "I'm leery of offering it to you. Frankly, it's not a position created to help a bored wife fill in a few hours. We don't need you to organize a thousand-dollar-a-plate dinner for us, then stand back and bask in the applause. We need our fund-raiser to constantly generate funds, to come up with new ideas month after month."

Caleb, Vicki realized, had really dropped her in it this

time. This was serious, nothing like a ceremonial board position. She wanted it so much she could hardly breathe but Helen was right. She had no experience or qualifications. Could she really do it? Then she remembered why Helen had come to see her in the first place. Because of Caleb. That he thought she was capable of this meant a great deal.

"I understand your concerns," she told Helen. "There's something else you need to know. I'm pregnant." She was a lawyer's wife—she knew it wasn't something she had to disclose, but she wanted every single fact on the table.

"That wouldn't matter if you were qualified. Like I said, it's a flexible position. And—" the other woman shrugged "—we don't have spare office space anyway so you'd be working from home."

"I want to do this." Vicki leaned forward, speaking with all her heart. "I know I'm not qualified and I know that to you I look like a spoiled wife, but I'd like to be more. Give me a chance."

Helen's eyes widened. "You're serious?" She continued to gaze at Vicki for another long moment. "Yes, I can see that you are."

"Could you give me a trial period? A month? If I can't cut it, I'll walk away and you don't even have to pay me."

"Tell you what. If you deliver, we'll pay you retroactively." Helen stood, clearly amused. "I should have known a man like Caleb Callaghan wouldn't be satisfied with a trophy wife. You're not what I expected."

"Thank you…I think."

"Thank me after you've seen the job you've taken on. We bleed money. I'll e-mail you the relevant details."

* * *

Victoria hugged Caleb the second he walked in the door for dinner.

"Hey," he said. "What's this?"

She looked up into his surprised face. "For being smart enough to help me out." Blinded by years of insecurity, she'd been fumbling in the dark.

Instead of taking advantage of her vulnerability to push his own agenda, Caleb had done something that showed her he was comfortable with her developing independence. It was the vote of confidence she'd barely dared to hope for. "I know you're busy so thank you for taking time out for me."

He shrugged and looked a little embarrassed. "It was just an idea. My way of apologizing for being such a fool last night."

"You're forgiven." She should have known he'd speak with actions, not pretty words. "How did you think of Heart?"

"You're so good with people I figured they could use you. So, did you take it on?"

Adoring him for his belief in her, she nodded. "*They're* taking me on for a trial period. Let's see if I can do it."

"You can. You can focus that stubborn will into work rather than on straightening me out."

Laughing, she led him into the dining room, where she'd set up a quick and healthy meal. "I'm going to keep working on that whether you like it or not."

"Damn." He patted her bottom affectionately as she sat down beside him.

Before, she would have pulled away in an effort to control her reaction to his nearness. Not anymore. She wasn't going to let Grandmother's poison ruin her marriage. "Eat." She kissed his cheek.

Halfway through the meal, he raised his head and asked, "Do you really think I'll be a bad father?"

She was startled enough to be completely honest. "I think you could be a great father but the way you're going, you might end up being an absentee one." When he remained silent, she pressed on. "Children don't only need things, they need a parent's presence, hugs and kisses and loving."

So do wives, she wanted to add. Wives needed love and attention most of all. A thousand diamond necklaces couldn't equal a moment of Caleb's love, a moment of being the center of his world.

Even if she found success in another arena, it would never be the thing her life revolved around. Caleb and her child would occupy that place. It was simply the way she was built. Perhaps because she'd never really had a family, her own small one meant everything to her. But her devotion also meant that each time Caleb put the firm above her, she felt it like a kick to the gut.

"Vicki, I don't know how to be a good father." It was a blunt statement, raw to the core.

Heart in her throat, she smiled. "And I don't know how to be a good mother." So far, she hadn't even done such a great job of being a good wife. "But I know one thing— as long as our child knows we'll always be there for her, she'll be okay."

That was a lesson Vicki had gleaned from the mockery that had been her childhood. All the other hurts would have been nothing if she'd known that she could run to her parents for comfort. "I know neither of us has great role models to follow but this is us, not anyone else. We can create the life we want for our baby." She had to believe that. Otherwise, her fear of messing up their child's life might just cripple her.

They didn't speak about the topic again, but when Caleb left to go back to the office, she saw the concentration on his face. He was thinking over what she'd said. She only hoped he wouldn't disregard it. A wife might be able to accept and understand, but a child's heart was much more fragile.

Caleb put down the phone after the last conference call with London and swiveled in his executive chair to stare out at the city lights. Silence reigned in a place that was usually buzzing with organized confusion. This particular deal was done. He'd sent his staff home two hours ago, confident he could tie up the loose ends.

It was a good thing tomorrow was Saturday. After the Donner crisis and then the problems today, everyone had been run ragged. Including him. As he looked out from his high-rise office to the beautiful lights segueing into the darkness of the sea, Vicki's words returned to haunt him.

Absentee father.

It was a term that applied to too many of the CEOs and lawyers he knew. Their children grew up under a loving mother's care if they were lucky, or under an indifferent nanny's if they weren't. Without their parents' guidance, he'd seen several of his acquaintances' children go off the rails.

Did he want his and Vicki's kids to turn to him one day and deny him any say in their lives because he'd never been there for them? No. He wanted the right to support their children, to help them grow, to provide encouragement and love. And he was intelligent enough to know he had to earn that right.

His sons or daughters would only respect what he had to say if he treated them as individuals worth making time for. Caleb knew that better than anyone. After the way his own father had treated him during his childhood, Caleb had never allowed Max any input into how he lived his life. Max had thrown away that right when he'd continually punished an innocent child for a mistake that had been made long before Caleb was born.

Vicki was right. Coming home for dinner would hardly be enough to nurture their children's love, to teach them their worth. He needed to be there for breakfast and dinner not only sometimes, but most of the time. He needed to drive his kids to school occasionally, to be around for sports games and school plays, for excited narrations of the day and even grumpy tantrums.

I know you're busy so thank you for taking time out for me.

The seemingly unrelated comment popped into his head, startling him. His wife had thanked him for making time for her. That seemed wrong. Following that thought, he found the link. So obvious. If occasional dinners at home wouldn't be enough for a child, how could they possibly be enough for a wife?

Unlike their child, or children, who'd have both a mother and a father, Vicki had no other husband to pick up the slack of Caleb's absence. If he didn't give her what she needed, no one would.

Even now, so soon after she'd begun to heal the sexual hurts between them, he'd let work get in the way of their journey. He'd pushed aside the importance of the steps they'd taken to find true intimacy and perhaps irreparably damaged the fragile trust that had grown the night he'd surrendered to her touch.

Picking up the photo of Vicki that sat on his desk, he ran his fingers over her laughing face. Jeans rolled up and hair tangled by the wind, she was standing ankle-deep in sand, looking mussed and happy enough to break his heart. It was his favorite picture of her…and it had been taken almost four years ago. His wife had stopped laughing long ago. And he hadn't been around enough to hear her silence.

Was it any wonder she'd wanted to divorce him? Sure, he'd been unhappy in their marriage, thinking that his wife didn't want him. As their marriage had crumbled, so had his dream—of a life with a wife who loved him absolutely, of a family as full of joy as his childhood one had been full of pain.

Then had come that business trip to Wellington four months ago when everything had shattered. The emotional destruction had been so bad that no matter how hard he'd tried, he hadn't been able to glue all the pieces back together.

But despite all that, he'd never felt abandoned the way Vicki must have. He'd always known that she was at home, waiting for him. That when he went to bed, his wife would be right there beside him, giving him another chance to repair the fissures in their relationship.

How many nights had Vicki slipped into a cold bed, aware that her husband wouldn't be home for hours yet? How many nights had she woken from a nightmare to find herself alone and without comfort? His gut twisted. Whatever the state of their marriage, he'd always been proud of the fact that he'd protected his wife and kept her safe from harm.

What rubbish!

He might have never raised a hand to her but there were other ways of causing pain and he'd been guilty of most of them. Every day and night that he hadn't been there when she'd needed him, he'd hurt her. And as for keeping her safe? What did Vicki do at night when storms blew the fuses? He'd never come home to find her waiting for him to fix things, hadn't even thought about it before now. But the answer was clear. She'd gone outside to the old-fashioned fuse box of their villa and done it herself.

What else did she do that he didn't know about? What else had she learned not to rely on him for? It was no longer enough that she'd agreed not to leave him, not when he'd glimpsed the fire she'd tried to contain her entire lifetime.

He was fascinated by the woman she'd revealed and he needed *her*, all of her. It was just starting to dawn on him that maybe more had been lost in those five years than Victoria's girlhood innocence.

Vicki woke the second Caleb slipped into bed beside her. She never really slept deeply until he was home, worrying about him on a subconscious level. Smiling, she snuggled into his warm body and started to drift back to sleep. She was aware that he was holding her tight, that there was something different about the intent in his body but she was too sleepy to figure out what.

"Vicki?" Kisses fell on her neck.

They felt so good that she cuddled closer. "Hmm?"

A big hand smoothed up her leg, bare under the rugby jersey she'd commandeered again. She shivered and the shadows of sleep started to fade. "Caleb?"

He answered by sliding that hand up her body until he cupped her breast. With a gasp, she came wide awake, belatedly aware that Caleb was naked beside her, his arousal pressed against her hip. Her first reaction was to freeze, to try to analyze what he was doing to her, to attempt to manage her reaction.

As if he knew exactly what was going through her mind, he whispered, "Do what you did last time."

Any hope of control evaporated at that request. She moved to run her hand down his body. Before she could, he tugged at the jersey and she raised her arms. A second later, he'd thrown the jersey aside and she was pressed against his heated skin, her fine-lace panties the only barrier between them.

"I can't touch you if you hold me like this," she whispered, acutely aware of the delicious roughness of his chest hair against her nipples, so sensitive these days.

"Why don't I have a turn instead?" He bit gently at her lower lip. Stroking his hand down her body, he lifted one leg and put it over his hip, leaving her scandalously open.

Fear clawed at her. Not fear of his loving, but of her own reactions. What if she let him down again?

"Stop thinking." One hand lay flat on her back, while the other moved between them.

"I can't help it." She was excruciatingly aware of the direction his hand was heading in. A second later, he slipped under the waistband of her panties to cup her intimately. She stilled, shocked at the riot of emotion within her.

"Tell me what you feel."

It was too hard to think, speak and keep her body under control at the same time. She bit down on her lower lip, trying not to let her breathing turn ragged.

"You know what I feel?" Caleb asked, spreading his fingers and starting to stroke her most delicate flesh. "I feel you hot and wet against my fingers, so silky soft and welcoming. I feel your body crying out for mine."

Eight

Vicki's mind was a buzz of sensation and sound. Caleb had never talked to her so explicitly before. He'd hardly talked at all when they'd made love. To her shock, she found she loved hearing his husky words, loved discovering another layer to his sexuality. Without her being aware of it, her body had softened against his as she concentrated on what he was saying.

"I think these pretty breasts of yours have gotten bigger." He shifted, without removing his hand from between her legs, until she lay on her back with him on her left. Pulling out the arm he had under her head, he propped himself up. "I'm going to turn on the light."

"No," she whispered. "Caleb, I can't…"

"I just want to see if I'm right about your breasts, sweetheart." The soft light of the bedside lamp hit her eyes. She blinked rapidly.

When she focused again, her throat dried up as her eyes went to that hand, stroking her so languidly that she felt herself melting. It was the slowest of seductions and she was starting to lose herself to it.

"They are," he whispered, leaning down to flick his tongue across one nipple.

She whimpered.

"Aren't they?"

The words spilled out of her. "They've swollen some."

He bit at the underside of her breast gently. "Does that hurt?"

"No." It felt good, so good. She wanted to ask him to do it again but she'd spent too much of her life remaining silent. A good child should be seen, not heard. A good wife should accede to her husband's requests but demand nothing herself.

"Do you want me to do it again?" he asked, holding out the temptation.

She fought back the voices of the past and reached for the promise of tomorrow. "Yes. Oh, *yes*."

He repeated the gesture on her other breast, murmuring, "I like the way you taste." Between her legs, his thumb found the small nub that could lead to exquisite pleasure. "What do you like? This?" He pressed his thumb hard. "Or this?" He rubbed his thumb in circles, then stopped. "You have to respond, honey." Slowly, he began to slide his hand out.

Desperate, she used one of her own hands to push him back down. Their eyes met and there was such sexual heat in his that she felt burned. Under her hand, he began to move again.

"This?" he asked again. "Or this?"

Their interlocking gaze was the most intimate thing she'd ever experienced. Running her tongue around a mouth gone dry, she nodded.

"Uh-uh." He shook his head. "You have to speak."

"Caleb," she begged.

"I promise you I'll like it." It was a lover's reassurance and a man's demand in one. "The way I liked it when you used your hands on me."

The words wouldn't come but she knew he wasn't going to go easy on her tonight. She had to ask for her pleasure. Instead of speaking, she moved her hand on his, showing him the movement that pleased her.

A slow smile spread across his face. "I'll allow that answer." Leaning down, he bit at her lip again. She arched up to further the kiss but he shook his head. "No kisses for you. You have to show me how you feel with the rest of your body. I promise I'll be endlessly patient."

She was dying, her breath coming out in pants. His fingers were driving her crazy. Taking her hand away from on top of his, she grabbed hold of one muscular arm. Her body was sheened in sweat but it was the heat in Caleb's eyes that she couldn't get enough of. He'd never looked at her this way in bed.

Tonight he was speaking to her with far more than his mouth. And she liked what she was hearing. She tried to kiss him again but he shook his head, staying frustratingly out of reach. Always before, she'd used her kiss to convey everything she felt but now she didn't have that outlet. Combined with the way he was touching her, it was pulling her remaining shreds of control to pieces. She dug her fingernails into his arms as her body arched toward him, seeking more.

One finger began to slide into her. "This?" His breath was hot against her ear. "Or this?" A second finger nudged at the swollen entrance to her body.

She pushed down against him, squeezing his body with

the thigh she had thrown over his waist. He heard and rewarded her by pushing those two fingers deep into her again and again. She felt the edge of something beautiful on the horizon but he stopped before she could reach it.

"Caleb, please. *Please.*" It was the first time in her life she'd begged for anything in bed. Part of her froze in shock at her own audacity, but the rest of her was too busy trying not to shatter as Caleb gave her exactly what she'd asked for.

Unable to kiss him, unable to release the wild sexuality riding her any other way, she screamed, her entire frame shaking with the shooting arcs of an orgasm so intense she thought she was going to black out.

She was barely aware of Caleb taking off her panties at last. When he rose up over her, she let him wrap her other leg around his waist. To her surprise, he didn't make any other move, waiting until she opened her eyes and focused on him.

His face was taut with sexual need but there was something very much like satisfaction in the curve of his mouth. "Time for round two."

Her eyes widened. She felt him nudge at her with his arousal but he didn't penetrate. Swallowing, she pushed her pelvis up, trying to entice him as she never had before. The tip of him lodged in her but despite her wordless plea, he wouldn't deepen the penetration.

"Not until you're with me."

Before she could say anything to that, he dipped his head to her nipple. The hard suction of his mouth sent sensation rocketing through every inch of her body. When he began to move his head away, she knew what she had to do. Caleb had taught her the rules of their very private game, given her the tools with which to fight her fear of doing something wrong.

Wrapping her arms around his neck, she held him to

her. He returned to his task with such obvious enjoyment it succeeded in destroying what little mind she had left. When he moved to her other breast, she felt her body buck upward. He pushed in another inch. And stopped.

Wanting to scream with the need to have him inside her, thick and hard, she ran the nails of her hands down his back. He jerked and raised his head, a red flush along his cheekbones. "You're not with me yet."

She wanted to beg for mercy but had a feeling Caleb wasn't going to give her any tonight. For the first time in almost five years, she had her wild lover back in bed with her, the one who'd always driven her half insane with need.

In the past, her own hunger had frightened her into silence, leading Caleb to leash his wild sexuality. But tonight the leash had been thrown aside and if she wanted to survive the ride, she had to let go and trust him to lead her over the edge.

When fear beckoned, she reminded herself of her decision—no more pretense, no more self-protection. Running her hand down one of his arms, she found his hand and brought it between their bodies to show him what she wanted. It was one of the hardest things she'd ever done but the payoff was the most exquisite pleasure. She felt the last thread of her control snap, throwing her into the dark hunger of their combined passion.

As her back arched under the circling strokes of Caleb's hand, he began to push into her at last. After two months of deprivation, her body was tight, her flesh hungry. She felt every inch of him, hot, hard and finally, *hers*. When he began to move, his rhythm was fast and deep, shocking another scream out of her as she surrendered to the inescapable glory of the heat between them.

At that moment, he kissed her. Starved, she reacted

like wildfire, giving herself up utterly to his loving. His spine went taut under her hands, his thighs locked and even as the flames licked at her, she felt him dive into the fire.

Vicki was smiling when she woke the next morning, her body deliciously sore but just as deliciously content. Snuggling into Caleb's arms, she'd started to drift back to sleep when her eyes registered the time. She sat straight up. "Caleb! Wake up, it's nine o'clock!" He absolutely hated being late.

Caleb pulled her back down and mumbled, "It's Saturday. Whole weekend off." She felt his body slip back into sleep.

Saturday? Yes, it was, she realized. Not that that had ever made much of a difference. Caleb always seemed to be at the office. She tried to think of the last time he'd taken off an entire weekend. She thought it might have been as far back as the four days they'd spent on Great Barrier two years ago.

A grin spread across her face. This meant Caleb was hers for two whole days! And she was free, too. The fundraising documents had arrived last night and she'd read them over. Ideas were bubbling inside her but she didn't officially start till Monday.

Unwilling to move out from under her husband's possessive embrace, she lay there and let her brain think up all sorts of things they could do together. The most attractive involved staying in this house, maybe even in this bed, for the two days. She wanted to laugh at her own giddy excitement, feeling like a child let loose in a candy store.

Having Caleb to herself for any length of time was one of her secret dreams, something she'd never asked for because she knew how busy he was—just because she had too much time on her hands, didn't mean she had the right to demand he keep her entertained.

But how she'd missed him, especially on the weekends when she'd gone out and seen couples strolling along the streets. She wondered if Caleb had heard more than what she'd said at dinner. Maybe, just maybe, her steamroller of a husband had heard the whispers of her heart.

Caleb roused to find Vicki's side of the bed empty. From the smell of coffee wafting into the bedroom, he guessed where she was. Smiling, he got out of bed feeling better than he had in years. Patience, he decided, was definitely a virtue. Look at what he'd been rewarded with last night.

Because he knew his wife's love of keeping all the windows open, he pulled on a pair of sweatpants before wandering out. Victoria was putting away a dish when he entered. The second she saw him, her eyes went huge.

"What?" He yawned, lifting his arms above his head in a lazy stretch.

Vicki stared at him, her lips parted. His sleepy brain finally figured out the matter with her. Apparently, his wife liked the sight of him sleep-mussed and drowsy. Maybe he should stop getting ready in the mornings before he came out for breakfast. With that thought, he bridged the gap between them and put his hands on her hips. "Good morning."

"It's almost noon." Her voice was breathy, her hands playing through the hair on his chest.

"Perfect time for almost-noon sex, don't you think?" After over two months of celibacy, his body had had a taste of paradise and wanted more. A lot more.

However, in spite of his sensual happiness, he wasn't blind to the fact that their marriage remained on shaky ground. Vicki had been right when she'd said they couldn't solve all their problems in bed.

What she hadn't said, what she probably couldn't see, was that if he was bad at sharing his darkest secrets, she was even worse. Though he'd never told her the ultimate shame of his birth, he'd tried to show her the reality of where he came from and how it had shaped him, scarred him.

But every time he tried to raise the same issues with her, she pretended she didn't know what he was talking about, pretended that her parents leaving her with Ada had had no impact. She might have confessed to him about her fears regarding intimacy but she wasn't even willing to *call* her relationship with Danica and Gregory a problem.

He didn't know how to make her see that those wounds needed to be lanced. It hurt her so much whenever he brought up the topic that he had no heart to force her to confront it. All he could hope for was that if he loved her body enough, she'd slowly start to trust him with her soul and her memories, too.

With that thought in mind, he dropped a hand down to curve over her pert bottom, covered by the soft fabric of her knee-length sundress—with the sun streaming brightly through the kitchen skylight, it was more than warm enough. "We don't want to lose our momentum."

She swallowed and he realized that he hadn't made love to her in the middle of the day for years. That was about to change. His erection was fierce and demanding. He wanted to be inside her, feeling her squeeze him as he moved slow and deep. Maybe he could get her to speak to him as she had last night—with her hands and the sensually explicit movements of her body. Or maybe she'd finally trust him enough to talk about far darker things.

As if she could read the images in his mind, those eyes got even bigger. "You look like you want to devour me."

"I do." He glanced past her shoulder to the window above the sink, which looked out over their small side yard and into their neighbor's property, a scandalous idea coming to him. It would shock Vicki's socks off but he was starting to understand that she'd always been far more gutsy than he'd given her credit for.

It was time to stop backing off and start showing her who he really was, start demanding things from her that he needed, sexually and emotionally. Before she could begin to suspect anything, he misdirected her attention by the simple expedient of kissing her.

"Mmm." She purred into his mouth, giving her all to the kiss as she always did.

Squeezing her bottom, he let her play with him, let her kiss him the way she wanted. He loved Vicki's kisses, especially the way she put her soul into every brush of lips and tongue. When she broke the kiss to caress his jaw with her lips, he made his move.

Kissing her neck, he turned her until she faced the window. Then he pushed her just a little. She instinctively braced herself against the edge of the counter, her gaze looking through the window above the sink and into the yard. He stroked her bottom, kissed her nape and grinned.

"Caleb," she whispered. "I need you." It was her way of telling him to get them out of the kitchen and into the privacy of their bedroom. But Caleb wanted to play.

Out of the corner of his eye, he saw their neighbor's back door open and someone step onto the patio. Before he could be spotted, he knelt down behind Vicki and slipped his hands under her dress to pull down her panties.

Startled, she almost turned but her attention was caught by Bill, their middle-aged neighbor.

She waved in greeting before hissing, "What are you doing? Bill—"

"Can't see me," he completed. "Pretend you're doing the dishes."

"While you do what?" She stepped out of her lace panties even while she protested.

Breathing in the scent of her, Caleb pushed up her dress, flattened one hand on her belly and tasted her like he'd been wanting to do since forever. From the first stroke, he knew he was a goner. She gave a soft shout and her whole body shuddered. "Caleb, I can't—"

"Sh." He blew a breath against her sensitive flesh. "Don't give away the game." Knowing he was being a merciless tease, he flicked his tongue along her exposed flesh, then nipped gently with his teeth. Her thighs trembled as the addictive flavor of her settled on his tongue and in his mind. This wasn't something he was going to get enough of, ever. Certainly it wasn't something he wanted to rush. The delight of her had to be savored.

Her breathing was jerky and he knew she was having trouble maintaining control. "Caleb—" Her sentence ended in an abrupt sob as he slid his tongue inside her. Her whole body started to shake.

Giving her a moment's relief, he pulled out and nipped at her bottom. "Is he looking your way?"

"No." She crumpled into his arms. "I'm going to kill you."

"First let me finish what I started." His fingers slid into her sweet flesh, stroking. "I want to taste you some more."

All her breath left her. She arched up and made no protest when he laid her out on the white tile of the kitchen floor, protecting her bare bottom by cupping it in his hands as he raised her to his lips. "Mercy," he said, as her scent ensnared him once more. But mercy was the last thing he wanted.

Victoria gave herself up to Caleb. He'd tried to love her this way at the start but she'd frozen, terrified of the passion that had begun to boil in her blood. Nothing he'd said or done had soothed. So he'd never asked that of her again.

A whimper escaped her throat as he suckled at her flesh, sending her nerves screaming. The muscles on her abdomen grew painfully taut as she closed her eyes to fight the building explosion. It was too much. She wouldn't survive.

"Let go," Caleb whispered, and she felt his hair brush her stomach as he pushed her dress farther up and kissed her navel. His kisses began trailing back down and this time, he wasn't playing. "Please let go."

It was the rough *please* that broke through the last of her reticence. With a soft scream, she felt her back lift off the floor as she let him overwhelm her senses. Behind her closed eyelids, lights exploded in a thousand colors. She couldn't stand the extremity of the pleasure, couldn't bear it.

Gasping, she tried to tell Caleb but he was already there, taking her lips in a kiss that gave her even more pleasure and yet also gifted her with the strength to ride the firestorm. Last night he'd been patient, so beautifully patient, but today he was asking her to hold up her end of the bargain, to give him the passion she'd withheld for so long. Lost in the hunger of his kiss, she could do nothing else but surrender.

When she finally blinked her eyes open, she found herself being carried to the bedroom. "Now you want a bed," she managed to tease.

Desire clouding his eyes, he grinned. "I didn't want to give you bruises. I'm feeling energetic."

"Caleb!" It was impossible to contain her laughter in the face of the unusual spark of mischief in his eyes.

He set her down gently on the bed. "I love your laugh." It was a quiet declaration.

Stunned, she held out her hands. He kept surprising her. Just when she thought she knew all she could about him, he came up with something so tender it broke her heart into a thousand pieces. "I miss you."

Holding her gaze, he shucked his sweatpants and got into bed beside her, one big hand stroking down her thigh as he bent his head to place a kiss on the exposed skin of her throat. Her dress was light but it felt too confining. When she wiggled, he raised his head. "What's the matter?"

"I want to take off this dress." She blushed. It was silly to blush after everything they'd done together but she'd always been shy about undressing in front of Caleb.

His eyes skimmed over her body. "I want to see you take it off." It was a challenge, but more than that, it was a request.

There was nothing she wanted more than to give him what he needed. But as Caleb himself had said, the habits of a lifetime couldn't be so easily forgotten. She wasn't some bold temptress; she was a woman accustomed to holding back.

Biting her lower lip, she pushed at his chest until he moved aside. In his eyes she saw nothing but patience. Once she was on her knees, she smoothed the dress over her thighs, feeling the heels of her feet against the bare skin of her buttocks. "Caleb?"

He spoke from behind her. "Yeah?"

"You have to keep helping me. Okay?" It was becoming easier each time she asked, because she was starting to learn that Caleb wouldn't deny her requests. Unlike the people who'd shaped her childhood, he'd never ignore her needs and tell her to toughen up.

"Always." He moved around until he was kneeling in front of her. "Close your eyes."

She let her lashes flutter shut. Then she lifted her fingers to the back zipper of her dress. Caleb's arms came around her as he helped her lower the fastening. She breathed in the warm, masculine scent of him and allowed her body to soften in pleasure. She'd come this far and was now tempted to push forward.

Caleb pulled away once the zipper was open and she knew what he was waiting for. Her husband wanted to see her undress in front of him. For most husbands and wives, it was an intimacy they took for granted. But for Caleb and Vicki it was so much more. Eyes still closed, she slid the straps down her arms and off her fingertips.

"You're wearing a bra." Caleb's voice was a caress in the darkness of her mind.

Not seeing him watching her made this easier. And yet, it turned the mood from hot to scorching. "They're starting to ache if I don't."

A fingertip traced the lace edges of her bra, shocking her with unexpected pleasure. "I like seeing you in satin and lace."

Her breath rushed out of her. Satin and lace. She'd never have guessed that her tough, practical husband would enjoy such a thing. "Shall I…?"

"Yes."

Reaching back, she undid the hooks and started to slide the straps down. Suddenly struck by remnants of her inhibitions, she stopped, far too aware of the dress pooled around her waist and the man watching her.

"I'll wait forever if you need me to."

How did he know exactly what to say to melt every one of her defenses? With a deep breath, she pulled off the bra and dropped it on the bed. Feeling more naked than she ever had before, she sat in place, listening, waiting, anticipating.

But nothing could have prepared her for the hot rush of Caleb's mouth on her breast. She cried out as he wrapped his hands around her waist and bent his head. The raw silk of his hair moving against her flesh clashed wildly with the scrape of his unshaven jaw and the tug of his teeth.

With her eyes closed, she was drowning in the sensations. She wanted to luxuriate in them. Her hands clenching in his hair, she lifted her lashes and found herself lost. Now she could see what she'd only felt—the golden heat of Caleb's skin, the sheen of wetness on her breasts as he moved his attention from one to the other, the utter pleasure on his face.

Tugging his head up, she tried to claim his lips in a kiss. When he wouldn't cooperate, she made a frustrated sound and uncurled her legs to grip him around the waist, her arms tight around his neck. She got her kiss. It had been a last desperate attempt to find some sort of anchor and it failed miserably as Caleb took merciless advantage of her wide-open position.

Pushing his hands under the bunched-up sundress, he started to slide her down onto him. She gasped. They'd never made love this way before—it felt as if he was invading her, going so far that she shuddered. "Too deep."

"Are you sure?" He paused and started to suckle at her neck.

She rocked toward him and felt him tense. Inside her body, he seemed to grow impossibly harder. Fascinated, she rocked again. This time, his hands tightened on her waist and he raised his head. "*Vicki.*" Grit out between clenched teeth, it was almost a growl.

She'd *never* made him sound that way. Suddenly he wasn't too deep. He was perfectly, wonderfully deep. Putting her hands on his shoulders, she held his gaze and pushed down. He groaned and his head dropped back, the tendons on his neck standing out in stark relief.

Scared by her own temerity but having starved for this moment, she started to move. Her fear of doing something wrong was nothing compared to the need she had to bring Caleb to the brink of ecstasy. She'd spent her marriage thinking she'd failed in bed with her virile husband. No way was she going to let this opportunity pass.

"Slow down." He buried his face in her neck, but didn't attempt to stop her quickening rhythm.

Taking her cue from his body, not his words, she did the opposite. His shoulder muscles tensed and untensed repeatedly as he ran his hands up and down her body. She could feel him riding the limits of control, feel him start to lose his mind and the woman in her rejoiced.

Tugging at his hair, she met his lips in a kiss designed to push him over the edge. She knew precisely what Caleb liked. So she bit at his lower lip, tugged it into her mouth, released it and did it again. His eyes were closed tightly by the time she began sucking on his tongue.

She was so into the kiss that she didn't realize he'd moved one of his hands between them until it was too late. He touched her just the way she liked, just the way he'd teased her into showing him the night before. She broke. But so did he.

Nine

Four hours later, they were walking through Mission Bay, having driven there looking for a nice place in which to have something to eat. After the wildness of their lovemaking, Caleb had helped her prepare a quick meal but they were both getting hungry again. Vicki couldn't care less where they ate—she was simply delighted to be out with her husband on a lazy Saturday afternoon.

"Do you want to grab something and go sit on the beach?" Caleb asked.

She looked across the road to the park abutting the sandy beach. "Sounds good. It's not too cold." Dressed in jeans and a thick, cable-knit sweater in sky-blue, she wasn't feeling the chill wind cutting off the sea.

Caleb pulled out the car keys from his jeans. "Why don't you go get the picnic thing you put in the trunk and

I'll grab something. Meet you over there." He pointed to a sunny spot. "Any preferences?"

"You choose." Taking the keys, she paused for an instant, then stood on tiptoe and quickly kissed him on the mouth before walking away. Such a small action but something she'd never have done before, believing public gestures of affection to be "inappropriate." Sometimes, she hated her grandmother, but she didn't want to think about that today.

Reaching the place where they'd parked the car, she opened the trunk and grabbed the picnic set she'd put in there months ago in the vain hope that Caleb would get the hint. That he'd remembered was a very good sign, she thought, locking the car. The small basket contained plates, eating utensils and a thin blanket to sit on.

She got to the beach before Caleb, her mind on the last time they'd done this. It had been the weekend after he'd won a big case three years ago. With a smile, she remembered him completely burning everything on the barbeque because she'd distracted him with her tiny, flame-red bikini—it had taken her hours to work up the nerve to expose the outfit he'd teasingly bought for her months before. They'd ended up eating meatless burgers because the isolated beach they'd gone to was too far from any shops. And for once, she'd known she'd pleased her husband.

Flicking out the blanket, she sat and put the basket on one edge to keep it from lifting in the soft breeze. As she waited for him to arrive, she people-watched. From the in-line skaters on the sidewalks to the families in the park, the area bubbled with energy.

One mother was throwing a ball to her laughing toddler, both of them wildly amused by the child's antics. Vicki found herself grinning along with them until her eyes fell on the man she guessed to be the father. He was sitting nearby but with a cell phone to his ear and an open brief-case beside him. Now and then, the woman would look over at him as if inviting him to join in the fun but he seemed barely aware of her or the child's presence.

A shadow fell across the blanket and a second later Caleb joined her, holding a pizza carton, cans of soda and what looked to be a foil-wrapped loaf of garlic bread. "What's got you so interested?" he asked.

"Nothing." She looked away but he'd already followed her gaze. Neither of them said anything as she opened the pizza box, propping the lid to keep the breeze from blowing sand into it. While she unwrapped the garlic bread, Caleb popped the cans of soda.

They'd both started to eat when Caleb spoke again. "Is that what you're afraid will happen with us?"

She couldn't be anything but honest. "Yes. But you're trying, honey, I know. I mean, we have this whole week-end."

"One weekend in a couple of months isn't going to cut it, is it, Vicki?" Those clear hazel eyes were so intense she felt as if he could see into her soul.

"A young child like the one over there might not notice so much," she said quietly. If he was willing to talk about this, she couldn't back away. "But a child who's going to school, who's playing on the soccer or hockey team defi-nitely will."

Putting another slice of pizza on his plate, she took a sip of soda before admitting something so painful she pre-ferred not to think about it. "I missed my parents every single day that they weren't there. I wasn't much into sports but I used to play the flute in the school orchestra."

She let herself remember the fading notes of memory, let herself remember the girl who'd looked out into the audience with such hope every single time. There was so much she still couldn't bear to face, but for the sake of their unborn child, she'd confront this particular hurt.

"Once in a while, we'd stage a concert. Grandmother would attend but she wasn't like the moms and dads who came with their video cameras, ready to record every moment, embarrassing their kids but showing them they were loved.

"She came so it couldn't be said that Ada Wentworth was neglecting her grandchild." She reached out to touch Caleb's cheek in a fleeting caress. "I don't want our child to feel like that, like an obligation. I don't want her to think that you're only in the audience because I forced you to come, that you'd much rather be at work doing something *important*."

Caleb put down his plate and linked his hand with hers, pulling her to sit close beside him. His face was turned toward the sea but she knew he was concentrating very hard on her words. "Work is part of who I am," he said. "I could never sideline it totally."

"I know that." She wished she understood why it was so important to him to keep striving to be better than the best. She knew it had something to do with his family but he'd always refused to talk about that part of his past. All she knew was that he had something to prove and he'd let no one stand in the way of that goal. Not even his wife.

Beaten by his stubborn will, she'd never pursued the issue but perhaps the time had nearly come—it was no longer her happiness alone on the line. "I don't expect you to push your work aside. All I want is for you to make room in your life for our child. Real room, not a moment here and there."

He didn't say anything else, but he'd listened. And while it wasn't enough, it was a start.

* * *

The sensual awakening that had begun on Friday night continued to develop throughout the weekend. It wasn't so much the physical pleasure they learned to give each other that was so important, but the emotions driving their desire to please each other. This time, they were determined to get it right. In bed and out of it.

The only sour note came as they were about to have coffee after dinner on Sunday night. Feeling supremely relaxed from the workout her husband had given her mere hours before, Vicki was smiling as Caleb went to pick up the phone.

A second after he answered, her smile disappeared. "Yes, Lara, of course it's me."

She put down the sugar bowl and walked over to join him. Touching his shoulder, she held out her hand for the phone. His gaze met hers and he shook his head. She knew why. Lara was probably going on and on and he didn't want to stress Vicki out.

His need to protect her didn't frustrate her, not now that she'd learned to stand up for herself when necessary. It had become a cherished gift, a sign that she was important to him.

Without warning, she grabbed the phone out of his hand and put it to her ear, slapping a palm on his chest to hold him off. Lara was in mid-rant. "Lara, this is Vicki."

A pause. "Why are you on the phone? Where's Caleb?"

"He wanted me to tell you the happy news." Vicki was furious at Lara for destroying their weekend, her temper hanging on by a very thin thread.

"What?"

She scowled up at Caleb when he tried to reach over her to get the phone. "I'm pregnant. Isn't that wonderful?"

Caleb raised an eyebrow at her tone, no longer attempting to snatch the receiver.

Another pause, and Vicki had the impression Lara was conveying the news to someone else. "Congratulations. Did you just find out?"

"No. We've known for a while."

"Thanks for telling us." Sarcastic.

Vicki smiled and made her tone so sweet, it was this side of cutting—she'd learned the rules of polite savagery from the best. "The thing is, Lara, you never ask about us when you call so we don't get the chance to share our news."

A small pause, as though Lara were deciding if her usually well-mannered sister-in-law was being bitchy. "Look, give the phone back to Caleb."

"I'm afraid he's unavailable." She leaned against him and wrapped one arm around his waist. His fingers started to play with the strands of her unbound hair, a silent statement that the call was now in her hands.

Buoyed by his support, she continued, "He's busy *earning* money to support our child. We really have to start saving for college from the start, don't you think?" A very long pause and in the background, harsh whispers. Her fingers tightened on the receiver. She knew exactly who was prompting Lara.

"He's my brother." The subtlest of threats.

"And he's the father of my child," she said softly, letting herself luxuriate in the feeling of something she'd barely dared to acknowledge before—Caleb's loyalty was hers, now and for always.

Though he didn't love her with the passionate devotion she knew his heart was capable of, though his work was the most important thing in his life, though he'd betrayed her in a way that had cut her to the core, he'd also shown her that she mattered. Mattered enough to fight for. And she was a woman who'd never mattered to anyone.

Caleb stiffened against her and she knew he was going to try and take over, having gauged what was going on. His ability to give her control obviously came to a screeching halt the instant he thought she might be hurt. Lord, she adored him, but he could drive her crazy. She pushed away and pointed at him to stay put. Eyes narrowed, he crossed his arms across his chest.

"You can't keep me from talking to my brother." Lara's voice started to rise.

"I would never try to." Vicki took a deep breath and pulled off the gloves. "As long as you don't make him unhappy when you call, you're free to talk to him. Can you do that, Lara?"

A long, almost dark silence, then the dial tone. Vicki sighed and put the phone on the wall cradle. "She hung up."

Caleb hugged her into his arms. "I don't want you dealing with my family. They can be—"

"No, Caleb." She tipped her head back and looked up at him. "I meant what I said. We fight each other's battles now. Don't take this away from me. I'm strong enough to support you."

He looked at her for a long, long time, a dawning pride in his eyes that nearly stopped her heartbeat. "You're very sexy when you're riled up, Mrs. Victoria Elizabeth Callaghan."

She laughed. "Uh-huh, coffee first. Then we'll talk." Backing away, she suited action to words and poured their drinks. Caleb kept teasing her with kisses on her neck until she finally pushed him into a chair and put his coffee on the table in front of him. "Behave."

He grinned and took a sip.

Shaking her head, she leaned her body against the edge of the table beside his chair, her mind on their earlier conversation. "What I don't understand is why your family is so hard on you. I mean, I know you chose a different path but no matter their philosophical problems with the capitalist way—" she rolled her eyes "—I'd have thought they'd be proud of you. Even my grandmother is impressed by your achievements and she's the harshest judge I know."

Caleb felt his jaw lock. "Yeah, well." This was one place he did not want to go.

She put a hand on his cheek, forcing him to look at her. "There's something more, isn't there?"

"Come on, sweetheart, let's just relax and have our coffee." He picked up his cup, wondering if she knew how pretty she looked in her pink sweater and jeans. She was what was important, not Lara and his parents. "I don't want to discuss my family right now."

He held his breath as he waited for her to drop the subject, to let sleeping dogs lie. But he'd forgotten how much things had changed.

"No, what you need to do is talk to me," she said, continuing to caress his cheek.

"There's nothing to talk about."

She dropped her hand but her eyes wouldn't release him. "Then why are you angry?"

"I'm not angry." Putting down his cup, he laid a hand on her thigh.

With another scowl, she put down her own cup and straightened from her leaning position. He thought she was accepting defeat. Then she threw one leg over him and straddled his lap, hands flat on his shoulders. "Talk to me."

"Maybe there are things I don't want to talk about." He'd put the crushing shame of his past behind him. There was no need to bring it all up. Not now. Not when their life was finally going wonderfully right.

"Tell me why they treat you this way." She frowned as he picked her up and put her aside before going to ostensibly refill his cup. "You can't shut down whenever you feel like it, Caleb."

His temper snapped. Thumping the cup on the counter, he faced her across the length of the room. "You're telling me I'm shut in? What about you?" It was a defensive strike and part of him was ashamed at using his skills at cross-examination to put Vicki on the back foot.

The truth was, he didn't want to talk about why his father hated him and his mother barely tolerated him. *Ever.* So he'd turned the spotlight on Vicki. But in spite of the reason driving him, he was also speaking the absolute truth.

Caleb looked more furious than Vicki had ever seen him. Despite all their fights up to this point, he'd never let his temper get this out of control. Right now, she could almost see the sparks in his eyes. What she couldn't understand was why.

"Me?" She pointed to her chest, hurt that he was bringing up her sexual deficiencies when she'd thought he'd begun to understand why she'd acted as she had. "I know I'm not great in bed but—"

He cut her off with a wave of his hand. "I'm not talking about sex."

"Then what?" She was truly confused but she wasn't about to let it show. Caleb was a good man but he was also a stubborn one who liked getting his own way. She refused to sit back and let him bulldoze over her. The last time she'd done that, it had almost destroyed their marriage.

"Christ, Vicki." He shoved his fingers through his already mussed-up hair, a remnant from their earlier loving. "Do you know how hard it is to get through that shell you've grown around yourself?" He shook his head. "You're like a damn hermit crab. Every time I ask too much of you, you withdraw into your protective walls." His eyes were tormented. "Do you know what it's like living with a woman who can shut you out without a thought? It kills."

She shook her head. "I don't. I've always tried to meet you halfway."

The word he said was sharp, blunt and so brutally explicit that she took a step back. Part of her wasn't sure she had the ability to deal with him when he was like this. The other part of her whispered that this was what she was fighting for—a husband who didn't hold himself back for fear that she couldn't handle him.

"I don't know what your family did to you," he said, "but it scarred you, even if you won't admit it. You're so terrified of letting anyone close to you, trusting anyone with a piece of yourself that you'd rather be alone."

"That's a lie!" she cried. "I'm fighting for us!"

"Are you? If I ask you questions you don't want to answer, ask you to face things you don't want to face, what will you do?" His jaw was clenched so tight, there were white lines around his mouth. "You'll go hide, get yourself under control, then smile at me in the morning as if nothing happened."

She couldn't speak, she was shaking so hard. Mutely, she reproached him. It wasn't true. It wasn't. "Maybe that was true before. But not anymore. I came to you," she whispered, reminding him of the night when she'd forced him to listen to her despite his anger.

"It's not enough to rip open your heart once and then seal it back up again, satisfied that you've filled your emotional debts."

"I don't understand." She was trembling.

His shoulders lifted as he put his hands on his hips. "Now that we're happy in bed, you feel like you can go back into that safe little shell where you live your life, where you don't have to deal with the fact that another person's needs might involve you making yourself vulnerable."

That broke her paralysis. "How can you say that? You know how much it hurt me when I thought I couldn't give you what you needed. I wouldn't have felt that way if I was closed off!" She was screaming, and she wasn't a woman who screamed.

His fists clenched at his sides. "But you didn't show it when it mattered, did you? You didn't talk to me about it. You just let the wound fester until divorce seemed the only option!"

She wanted to argue but couldn't. He was right. Even now, she still kept secrets—the most damaging, painful kind of secrets. She'd tried not to think about it, tried to put what he'd done with Miranda behind her, but his infidelity continued to be a bleeding cut inside of her, something that wore away at the soul of their marriage. Yet she couldn't bring herself to speak about it, couldn't bring herself to lay her heart open to the blinding hurt she knew awaited.

"How many things are you never going to talk to me about because they're too hard to face?" His eyes were a maelstrom of emotion. "Do you know why I'm really mad? It has nothing to do with our problems in bed."

"Then what?" she asked, terrified she knew the answer.

"Marriage is about mutual trust, Vicki. Mutual support. It's a partnership, but you're only willing to embrace the pieces of that partnership that suit you. It's easy for you to focus on helping me confront my scars. That way, you don't have to look at your own."

Vicki couldn't speak. Word after word, Caleb was destroying the tools of survival that had helped her grow up without a mother and father, without any loving attention.

"You ask me about my family but when have you ever spoken about yours? Last year, Danica came to visit and you cried for a week after she left but *you wouldn't tell me why.*" His voice broke. "Do you think I don't know how much you keep inside? How much you bury so you won't have to admit you were hurt?"

A sob caught in the back of her throat. "Am I that weak?" she whispered. "That scared of dealing with the past?" Her hands lifted to her mouth.

The agony in Vicki's eyes devastated Caleb. Guilt awakened but he wasn't willing to retreat. This was the closest she'd ever come to speaking about her secrets. "You're not weak." Crossing the distance that had separated them during the course of the argument, he drew her hands away from her mouth.

"But I'm so afraid, Caleb. So terrified."

"Of what, sweetheart?" A fist was clenched around his heart, squeezing the life out of him. He was as much to blame as her for their situation. He'd helped her hide, helped her pull away from everything that might be too much, gone so far as to restrict his needs to what he thought she could handle.

Yes, sexually, they were starting to come into sync but what about emotionally? She remained so far from him, so wary of giving him everything. All the touches in the world couldn't hide the fact that she'd never once told him she loved him.

He used to whisper love words into her ear, but never had she said them back. This time, he wasn't going to lay his heart on the line. Not without her taking the same chance, which meant she had to break free from the past. "What are you afraid of?" he repeated when she remained silent.

"Of being thrown away again."

The almost inaudible words defused his anger. He tugged her to him and held her tightly. She wrapped her arms around his waist, shaking so hard he thought she might break. "Don't you ever be afraid of that." He ground out the words. "Ever. You hear me?"

She didn't answer, her fingers digging into his flesh. He kissed the top of her head, and tried to warm away the shivers racking her body.

"I will never walk away from you." His tone left no room for argument. "I keep my promises. And on our wedding day, I promised you forever."

She let out a choked whisper. "I n-never knew I was s-so afraid," she said against his chest. "I never wanted to see it. If I didn't look at that fear, I d-didn't have to think about my parents deserting me."

"They care for you in their own way." Having met both Gregory and Danica, he knew what he was talking about. "They're simply not good parent material."

"How could they leave me behind like that?" she asked, her voice broken. "Just leave me with Ada and drive away to new lives? Like I was an unwanted pet. How could they do that, Caleb?"

Tears threatened to clog Caleb's throat. He fought them with every ounce of strength he had, wishing he could fight Victoria's demons for her. But all he could do was hold her safe and let her release her anger, her pain, her sorrow.

After what seemed an eternity, she spoke again. "My mother used to call me her little angel. I remember sitting beside her vanity watching her put on makeup and thinking her the prettiest woman alive." Raw emotion layered every word. "She'd tell me that I'd grow up to be exactly like her and that when the time came, she'd show me how to make myself even prettier. Sometimes, she'd put a little nail polish on my toes and I'd feel like a grown-up."

He ran his hands down her hair, feeling it so soft against his skin, so delicate. Like Vicki's heart. A heart that had been trampled on, bruised.

"Then one day, she packed up my clothes, drove me to Ada's and waved goodbye. My father had already left months before. He'd never been that close to me so it didn't hurt as much, and after a while, I got used to it. I still had Mom and moms don't leave.

"For the longest time, I thought she was going to come back. I used to sit on the front steps waiting for her." Vicki pulled back a little and he allowed her space. When she raised her hands to wipe her cheeks, he shook his head and took over the job. Her lips trembled as she tried to smile.

"Sweetheart," he said, broken by the sight of her tear-streaked face. "Enough. It's enough." He hated himself for pushing her into this while hiding his own secrets. What kind of a coward did that to his wife, the woman he'd sworn to protect?

Instead of obeying, she touched his jaw in a tender caress. "Ada finally had enough. Two months in she told me that the w-whore wasn't coming back, that she was more concerned with spreading her legs for her new lover than she was with her child."

Caleb was so angry that his hands shook as he cupped her cheeks. "She's a bitter old woman who should never have been given the care of a child. Don't let her words poison your life."

Vicki's tentative calm seemed to fracture completely at his words. Giving a ragged cry, she struck at his chest with her fists. "But my mother left me with her! She knew exactly what Ada was like and still she left me behind. Sometimes I hate Mother so much I scare myself."

She collapsed. If he hadn't caught her, easing her down, she would've hit the floor hard. Tugging her into the V of his thighs, he held her as she cried angry, raw, wrenching sobs. They were so violent that he worried for the child in her womb.

In the aftermath, he'd learn whether she had any room in that bruised heart to take a chance on him.

Ten

Vicki woke to darkness. She blinked and moaned, real-izing she was alone in the master bedroom. Her nose was stuffy, her eyes dry and her mouth felt as if it had been filled with cotton wool. Rubbing her hands over her face, she sat up slowly then stumbled to the bathroom.

"I look like hell," she said to her reflection after throw-ing cool water on her face.

"You look beautiful." The quiet statement had her spin-ning around. Caleb stood in the doorway, dressed in his favorite dark gray sweatpants.

"Where were you?"

"I was working in the guest room." He jerked his head in that direction. "I didn't want you to be alone when you woke."

She gripped the edge of the sink, not sure she wanted him to see her like this. This vulnerable. This needy.

You'll go hide, get yourself under control, then smile at me in the morning as if nothing happened.

Breaking the habit was beyond difficult. "I feel like I've been scraped raw." It was an emotionally honest statement.

"You have." Caleb fully entered the room and put his hands on her shoulders. Their eyes met in the mirror. "God, baby, you scared me. So much rage, so much pain." The use of an endearment he rarely used for her showed her exactly how shaken he'd been. "You've been burying it inside since you were four years old. It's been killing you bit by slow bit." His arms wrapped around her shoulders.

"And you with me," she whispered, reaching up to touch one of his hands.

He dropped a kiss on her cheek. "We'll both heal because neither of us is a quitter."

Not like your parents.

The words were unspoken but she heard them bright as day. "I'm not so sure I'm as strong as you think," she admitted.

"Let me be the judge of that." His body was a warm wall of protection at her back. "You grew into the woman you are today despite Ada trying to suffocate your spirit. To me, that makes you a miracle."

The words were precious gifts to her. She used them to patch some of the holes left from her emotional storm. "Until death do us part." It was a vow stronger than the one she'd had the capacity to make on her wedding day.

To her surprise, he grinned. "If you think I'm ever letting you go, you've got another think coming. Me and God have an understanding."

The comment snapped the solemn mood and she found herself smiling, then giggling. "Caleb!" Turning in his arms, she hugged him tight. He was her husband and her strength. He was also her greatest weakness. It was time to stop running from that truth and embrace what it implied about her own needs and desires.

The next day, she decided there was something they had to finish. She found him in the attached garage changing the oil in her car. To her surprise and delight, he'd taken Monday off to be with her. Watching him, she wanted to sigh in pride. Her man was sexy as anything wearing those old jeans that were almost falling off his hips, a streak of grease across his chest.

"Can you pass me that rag, honey?" he said as he ducked out from under the hood.

She handed it to him, watching him wipe his fingers. When he gave her a slow smile, she knew what was on his mind. Shaking her head, she stepped back. "Not until we finish what we started last night."

He frowned. "I think you've hurt yourself enough for one week."

That his first thought concerned her welfare was all the impetus she needed. "We've laid my cards out on the table. What about yours?" A part of her whispered that there was one more huge thing they still hadn't even come close to discussing, but she shushed that voice.

After what he'd said to her last night, she had no more doubts that Miranda was gone from his life. That weekend in Wellington had clearly been an anger-fueled mistake on his part and one she could understand, no matter how much it hurt. It was time to truly forget about it and move on. For all their sakes.

He closed the hood. "There's nothing to talk about."

She reached out with one hand and touched his lower back. "Please, Caleb."

Shame and need combined to make an explosive combination. Caleb turned on her, forcing her to break the contact. "What? It's some sort of trade? You talk and then I have to?" It was the instinctive striking out of an injured animal, harsh and without thought to the damage it might do. The response came from the part of him that had been *hurt* in a way no child should ever be hurt. That part didn't want to suffer anymore.

Vicki drew back as if he'd hit her. "Actually, I only wanted to help you like you helped me." Her whole body was stiff. "But clearly I don't know the rules. I'm sorry I was stupid enough to come out here thinking we were finally ready to give an honest partnership a go." Teeth obviously clenched, she started to walk away.

Even the wounded animal inside him had no defense against his intrinsic need to protect her from distress, especially when he was the cause. It didn't matter if the cost of protecting her would be seeing shame dull her eyes. Losing her respect was his worst nightmare, but that was no excuse for the way he'd lashed out at her today *and* yesterday. No excuse for cowardice.

He manacled her wrist to stop her. "Sweetheart, don't."

"Don't what? Expect more from you than you're willing to give?" she asked without looking at him. "Don't ask for your trust?"

Tugging her back, he tumbled her into the V of his legs as he leaned against the car. She shifted to look at him at last, her eyes holding more anger than sadness. He ran his hand over her arm. "Can't you just accept that there are parts of my life I don't particularly want to talk about?" It was a last-ditch effort.

"Could you accept it of me?" she asked. "What if I told you, 'Caleb, here are the parts of my life that you're invited into and those parts over there, the painful, horrible parts, those you don't even get to know about.'" She crossed her arms. "Is that what I should've done last night? Should I crawl back into that shell you so hate and stop bothering you?" Her gunshot-fast words smacked him in the heart.

"You used to be so non-confrontational."

"Do you want that woman back?"

He squeezed her waist. "Are you kidding? That woman barely talked to me." Though he made his tone light, he was terrified. What if Vicki never looked at him in the same way again?

At last, she smiled. "When did you learn how to be charming?"

That was the one thing no one had ever accused him of. "When I found out you can't get enough of me." He told himself to have faith in his wife's heart—she'd never look down on him. But right now, the reasonable adult wasn't in charge. Instead, it was the vulnerable boy who'd grown up being treated as if he were something dirty.

Her laugh filled the garage, destroying the anger that had colored the air an instant before. It made him hope. "Talk to me, Caleb. If I don't know all of you, then I'll always feel like I'm letting you down and I've done enough of that. No more. *Talk to me.*" The last words were a whisper filled with so much need that denying her became impossible.

He let out a breath and started speaking, trusting his wife as he'd never trusted another human being. "You've met my parents, seen how they live, their philosophy in life."

"Art is everything and rules are for other people," Vicki said, encapsulating the creed that Max and Carmen lived by.

"Including the rules about fidelity and the meaning of

marriage." Caleb could see comprehension start to dawn in her eyes. "They had an open marriage before I was conceived."

"Other lovers?" His wife's innocent eyes went wide. Her view on fidelity and loyalty was one of the things he adored most about her. She'd tried to divorce him but he knew absolutely that she'd never, not once, even thought about cheating on him.

He hadn't been as strong. Broken by her apparent dislike of being intimate with him, he'd wanted to take a lover, to show her that he *was* desired. That she'd never discovered his lapse was something he'd be forever grateful for.

"Yes." He confirmed her guess. "Apparently they were very mature about it. Then my mother got pregnant after she'd been with Max and another man…at the same time. She had no idea who the father was until I was born." The shame of his origins burned like acid. "Max was very accepting and supportive. On the surface, it was business as usual."

"But?"

"But soon after my birth, it became obvious I wasn't his—our blood types don't mesh." The discovery had destroyed the pretense and opened the door to hatred. "Even as a small child, I knew he couldn't stand the sight of me."

How did anyone ever learn to accept that the man he'd been raised to see as his father only saw him as a loathed mistake? "They never hid my origins from me and soon enough, I figured out why he hated me so much."

"What about your mother?"

"She had to make a decision very early on and she decided to stick by my father. I was pretty much left on my own. There was no violence. But there was no love, either." How many times had he walked into a room only to watch his father walk out? As an adult, he couldn't understand how Max could have behaved that way to a child, someone who would have worshipped him given the slightest encouragement.

It was pathetic how much Caleb had craved Max's love. "I wanted my father to be proud of me but I eventually realized that nothing I did would ever make him happy. I'm a living reminder that another man touched his wife, that he not only allowed such a thing to happen, but also participated. Nothing I do will erase that truth."

"Oh, darling." Vicki kissed him gently. "How could they have done that? Blame you for their choices? You were a baby, an innocent."

Looking into blue eyes filled with anger on his behalf, he felt long-buried injuries surface with agonizing fury. But hope whispered through the pain. "Maybe it would've been better if my biological father was a stranger but the thing was, he wasn't. At the time, he was Max's best friend. We're carbon copies as far as looks go."

"You've met him?"

"He dropped by a few times over the years to see 'his boy.' I hated those visits because after he'd gone, everything would get worse. Max...I swear that sometimes, he wished he could kill me and remove me from his sight."

She made a sharp sound and her hands clenched on his biceps. "Why didn't you go away with your biological father?"

"Wade? Wade is a drifter, a drunk with no fixed address and nothing but a battered guitar to his name. The real reason he came to see me was that he knew he could get a few dollars out of Carmen when Max wasn't looking. I haven't seen him for almost ten years, though I heard from Lara that he's shacked up with someone down south."

"What about Lara?"

"That's what hurts the most. When we were kids, I was the one who looked after her, made sure she ate and had baths. But as she grew older and recognized that she was the clear favorite in the family, she began to mimic Max and Carmen. After a while it wasn't imitation anymore."

It had ripped him to pieces to see rejection in the eyes of the very girl whose knees he'd kissed after a hundred falls. Sometimes, he thought it was Lara who'd done him the most damage. He'd become immune to Max and Carmen but he'd been wide open for her knife to the heart.

And there it was, his whole sordid history. Conceived in prurient lust, he had a biological father who was a worthless drunk, a stepfather who despised him and a mother who'd chosen to emotionally abandon him.

Yet he'd dared to dream, to reach for someone so pure and bright, someone untouched by the tawdriness that was his legacy.

Most of their marriage he'd spent grateful that Vicki didn't know the truth of where he'd come from. Sure, she'd seen that he had humble roots, but she hadn't known the true extent of his degradation. He'd never wanted her to feel shame at being Caleb Callaghan's wife, never wanted to destroy the shine in her eyes.

"We're the same," she whispered.

It was the one response he wasn't prepared for. "Vicki?"

"I might be the biological offspring of my parents but that's only by chance. They serially cheated on each other. Grandmother placed the sole blame on my mother, but I'm not stupid. I listened to what the servants gossiped about. My father was, and still is, known for his penchant for young secretaries." She shrugged. "The one good thing you can say about them is that they divorced and didn't make me miserable by keeping me between them."

"No, they let Ada do that." His anger on her behalf momentarily overcame his shock at the way she'd placed them both in the same category. "They'd have done better to put you in boarding school. At least that way you wouldn't have had to grow up listening to constant emotional abuse."

To his surprise, Vicki laughed and hugged him. "Thank you for being angry for me." Pulling back, her face grew serious. "If you can be angry for me, I'm allowed to be furious for you. No more, Caleb. I've drawn the line. We ensure Lara's kids get taken care of but everyone else is on their own. I won't have them acting like it's their right to ask you for money, for support, when all they've ever given you is pain."

He'd never imagined the moment would come when his wife would fashion herself *his* protector, accepting his darkest secret with honest simplicity that gave him the tools to do so himself.

The pain of his parents' rejection wouldn't disappear overnight, but he knew it would never again be the razor-sharp anguish he'd grown used to. He'd been accepted by someone far more important to him than a man and woman who'd long ago lost the right to his respect, someone he adored with every breath he took. "Thank you, sweetheart."

She shook her head. "No thanks necessary. We'll look after each other. You save me from Queen Ada and I'll save you from Max, Carmen and Lara. Deal?"

He grinned at her use of the nickname he'd created for her grandmother, even as he thanked God for her. It was clear that the impact of her own emotional upheaval was still surging through her, but equally obvious was her fierce desire to ensure his happiness. How could he not be crazy about her? "Deal."

That Tuesday, Victoria sent Caleb off to work with a smile and a kiss. She loved that she could do that—kiss her husband goodbye with every ounce of passion she had in her and not worry that she was doing the wrong thing.

"Be home for dinner," she ordered.

"Yes, ma'am." He grinned and blew her a kiss as he walked out to the car, a lightness to his step she'd never before seen.

Laughing, she returned the gesture then walked back into the house to get started on her work for the charities. "My work," she said, doing a little dance. Her whole body echoed the lightness in Caleb's step. It felt as if a cloud had lifted from both of them.

Shadows continued to linger but the festering darkness had been confronted and banished. Maybe one day they'd speak about Miranda, but now that they'd finally become a solid unit, it seemed foolhardy to bring it up. It was done, and given Caleb's views on fidelity, he'd probably punished himself a hundred times over for his slip. For the sake of their child, she had to wipe away that last remnant of pain and move on to other things, such as her new job.

She had no illusions the work would be easy. It might even be impossible. But she was going to try, and no one could ever laugh at her for that, for attempting to be a woman she could be proud of. Before she could earn Caleb's respect as a partner, she had to rebuild her own self-image, had to become happy with who she was as an individual apart from her husband.

She wasn't a business or legal whiz, nor was she artistically gifted, but she had a way with people. This job was simply a tool to help her understand and appreciate her own strengths.

Picking up a few of the documents she'd printed out from Helen's e-mails, she started to read. Some of the technical, money stuff she put aside. She wasn't too proud to ask Caleb for help, aware that he looked at a lot of financial reports during his working day. However, it boosted her confidence when she quickly grasped the majority of the issues.

Helen was right. The charities bled money and, unfortunately, there was no way to plug the gaps. These operations were already run on a shoestring and a prayer—injections of cash at regular intervals were a necessity. As Helen had said, not one costly dinner, but a steady stream of money.

Vicki took out a piece of paper and started noting some names. She knew people who knew people and those people had lots of influence in the right places. Perhaps all that mingling was about to come in handy.

Caleb cleared his files in record time and managed to make it home before six. He had no intention of letting Vicki down, not after everything they'd gone through the previous weekend. If he was being honest, part of him wanted to make sure she hadn't changed her mind about him.

The sudden vulnerability was uncomfortable but he knew the look in Vicki's eyes as she welcomed him home would make it bearable. However, when he arrived, it was to find her closeted in her study with dinner nowhere in sight. After a flare of irritation, he dialed out for Chinese. Then he headed to her.

"Busy?" he asked, standing in the doorway of the room she used as her study and sitting room. In the past, she'd often retreated here and he'd felt shut out of her life. Though he knew this wasn't the same, the memories that came with the room were enough to aggravate the already raw edges of his emotions.

She looked up, her distracted air clearing. "Oh, you're home." Then she frowned. "What time…oh my God! Give me a few minutes to throw something together for dinner."

He caught her flustered body as she tried to rush by him. "I'd rather you spent that time kissing me."

"Caleb! Dinner—"

"—has been taken care of."

Looking guilty, she dropped her head on his chest. "Time got away from me. This fund-raising job is so interesting. I've been putting together a few ideas. I really want them to hire me when the month is up."

He'd never seen such excitement on her face. "Tell me about it over dinner." Then he kissed her the way he'd been wanting to do since he'd walked through the door.

She sighed and returned the kiss, using her mouth in ways that she'd learned pleased him. Groaning, he tightened his embrace, feeling his arousal grow. Forget about dinner, he thought, what he really wanted to gorge on was his wife's beautiful body. And it was about so much more than sex. Without this physical contact, both of them would flounder in their emotional healing. He'd learned that the hard way when he'd stifled his own tactile nature.

"I hate this room," he murmured into her mouth, telling her another truth he'd kept inside for too long.

She undid his tie. "Why?" The tie was flung to the side, her fingers on the button at his collar.

"You used to hide from me in here." It had compounded

his feelings of rejection to know that his wife couldn't bear his presence. He still wasn't completely recovered, still not certain she wouldn't withdraw into her shell if he asked too much of her.

She didn't deny it. "Want to make new memories?" Pressing a kiss to the skin she'd bared at his throat, she smiled. "I could do with some happy ones, too. I think that side of our ledger is in serious debit."

He felt something in him lighten. "They'd have to be red-hot." When he pulled at the bottom of her turtleneck, she lifted her arms and let him peel it off. "Blazing hot." He ran his fingers over the satiny straps of her bra.

Her eyes were soft with welcome but it was with her actions that she spoke. She slipped button after button from his shirt and spread the sides open. "You are so perfect, Caleb. Sometimes it feels like you were created from my dreams."

No one had ever said anything so wonderful to him. No woman had ever looked at him as if he was everything she'd ever desired. Vicki wasn't merely accepting him, she was thanking him for coming into her life.

Lost, he began to slide one strap off her shoulder.

The doorbell pealed in the distance.

"Dinner?" Vicki's disappointed expression did nothing to quieten his arousal.

"Bad timing," he muttered. "Stay here. I want to eat my dinner off you."

Buttoning a few buttons on his shirt, he let the tails hang out as he walked to the door. In the minute that he was gone, he knew Vicki would cover up despite his request. The last thing he expected to see when he returned to the study was his wife waiting for him…naked.

She was lying on the sofa, her body flushed and pink,

her eyes turned to the doorway. Against the deep blue backdrop, she looked like a glistening pearl but there was nothing cold about her. This woman invited touch, invited seduction. And he knew it was an invitation she would only ever extend to him.

He dropped the take-out box on the floor and tore the buttons off his shirt in an effort to remove it. She looked so delicious he wanted to lick her straight up from her curling toes to the blushing tips of her hair. "Why?" he rasped, crossing the distance to kneel beside the sofa, unable to wait long enough to get rid of his pants.

"Red-hot memories," she whispered, face pink from her blush.

He knew exactly how difficult this was for her, how much it must have cost her to let go of all the things she'd been taught for so long. How scared she must be that she'd done something that would turn him away from her. He'd never expected her to take such a chance and expose herself to rejection so soon after she'd broken through that shell of hers. And yet she had. For him. For *them*. To balance out the happiness side of their ledger.

He put one hand on her stomach, near the soft triangle between her legs. "Sweetheart, this is beyond hot. You're burning me up."

Some of the tenseness evaporated from her expression. "Why are you…?" She waved a hand at his pants.

"Because I think my very brave wife deserves some pleasure and if these come off, I'm afraid I won't last." He slid his hand down and tugged gently at her curls.

Her breath caught. "It's so bright."

"It's perfect," he told her, glorying in his ability to see every inch of her body. "I want to watch you come for me." He'd never talked so erotically to her before, had never been confident that she could take it. Even now, he watched her eyes, ready to pull back if she looked even slightly uncomfortable.

She swallowed and then spread her thighs just the tiniest bit. The musky scent of her arousal washed over him. He moved until he was able to take one of her legs and place her foot on the floor in front of him. She watched him drink her in, her pulse a thudding beat against his body.

"Hook your other leg over the back of the sofa." He wondered if he was pushing her too far.

She bit her lip. "Why don't you turn off the lights?"

"I want to see you spread out for me, wet and ready. I want to see what I'm tasting. Men are very visual creatures," he teased, telling her that he'd treasure her response.

To his surprise, she gave a soft laugh. "It's not only men." Her eyes skimmed over his bare chest. "Can we do it in stages?"

He'd never dreamed they'd ever come this far, physically *and* emotionally. The trust that had forged between them over the past few days was affecting every corner of their life. Who knew where it would lead? "Step by slow step." Pushing gently at the leg on the floor, he spread her just a little bit more. On the sofa, she bent her other leg at the knee.

When his hand stroked the silky skin of her inner thigh, she gasped and he saw her fingers clench on the thick fabric that covered the sofa. With his free hand, he repeated the caress on her other leg. Her whimper meant everything to him. Slowly, she was starting to talk to him in bed, starting to give him more than her body alone.

"I'm going to kiss you," he warned her, looking up until she met his eyes. "I'm going to savor every sweet inch of you. And then I'm going to do it again."

She swallowed and lifted her foot off the sofa. He was so hard that he felt as if he would break. He slid one hand down to her calf and helped her get the leg over the back of the sofa. He was almost afraid to look at the beautiful sight of her lying open and ready for him, terrified of the hunger that had him in its grip.

He looked at her face to find that she'd closed her eyes, as if to watch him adoring her would be too much to bear. His own hands were shaking. Taking a deep breath, he allowed himself to look at what she was offering. Need overwhelmed him in a violent wave.

With a groan, he slipped one hand below her bottom and lifted her to his bent head, his free hand on the inner face of one thigh. She shuddered as he blew hot breath against her open lips and her entire body went taut with anticipation. Flicking out his tongue, he teased the nubbin hidden in her curls.

"Oh!"

The cry acted like lightning in his bloodstream. He bent to his task in earnest, treating her sweet flesh like the most exotic of delicacies, something to be enjoyed slowly and with the greatest attention to detail.

"Caleb!" It was a sobbing scream.

"Yes, honey," he said, against her. "Let go for me." He kissed her again, using his mouth to wring another scream from her before her body started to ripple in climax. Drawing back, he did as he'd said he would—he watched her shatter from his touch, watched her back arch, her breasts flush, the nipples standing out in sharp relief as she rode the waves of pleasure until there was no breath left in her.

Only when she was gasping in recovery did he stand and strip himself. Putting one knee on the sofa between her spread thighs, he took the leg she'd hooked around the back and urged her to wrap it around his hips. It put her in the perfect position for his ultimate enjoyment.

Her eyes fluttered open a second before he slid his hand beneath the thigh wrapped around his hips, held her tight and pushed. Slow and deep. The maleness in him was very aware of the precious life inside his wife's body and he took every care with her, pushing in and out with a deliberation that made her buck toward him. He did it again and again. And again.

Until Vicki screamed and he had no choice but to follow her over the edge.

Eleven

"I love this room," her husband whispered in her ear as he handed her his shirt.

She pulled it on, blushing. "Caleb, that was... I can't believe... Oh, just get the food."

Grinning, he kissed her once then went to pick up the fallen box, which was amazingly still in one piece. Her mouth dried up at the sight of his beautiful body laid bare for her perusal.

As he returned to her, he raised an eyebrow. "Don't look at me like that. You've finished me off completely, you insatiable woman." He put the box in her lap and looked around until he found his briefs and pants.

"Are you sure?" she teased, put at ease by his irreverence. She wanted to groan as she watched him zip the pants but leave the top button undone. Her husband was the most unbelievably sexy man she'd ever met and she craved him. Her body was sated but she continued to want to touch, to adore. Somehow she didn't think it was the fault of her misbehaving hormones—not when she'd wanted him like this forever.

He sat beside her. "Feed me, woman." The laughter in his eyes had her making a face at him.

"It's almost cold." She opened the box and lifted out a container of fried rice.

"And you are hot." Leaning over, he bit her earlobe.

She giggled and handed him the container. "Behave." But she didn't really mean it. The last thing she wanted was for her husband to behave, to go back to the cool formality with which he'd once treated her. This was what they'd been like in the very beginning, before everything had gone wrong.

The difference was that now a deep vein of loyalty ran between them, a shockingly intense commitment Vicki wasn't quite ready to explore. But at least she was no longer hiding from his needs or her own.

As they ate, the talk turned gradually to Vicki's ideas for Heart. Caleb had every intention of being involved in this new part of her life. There would be no more walls between them, no matter how exposed that made him feel. Compared to the agony of isolation, naked vulnerability was almost easy. Almost.

"So," she said after finishing her sweet-and-sour chicken, "I thought if we could get a spot on that radio show, we might be able to lure in the people we need most."

"Sounds like you'll be busy."

The joy on her face faded. "You don't think it'll work? Me doing this and the baby? I mean, day one and I forget dinner—"

He halted her by the simple expedient of a kiss. "I

didn't mean anything like that. It'll work. You aren't superwoman so we'll get a cook and cleaner, but it'll work."

"No nanny," she declared, mule-faced. "I'll raise our baby."

"No nanny," he agreed.

"Caleb," she took a deep breath, "I know how important it is to you that I be at home, so thank you for supporting me in this."

Surprised, he said, "I never expected you to be a housewife if that wasn't what you wanted."

"But you prefer it. Tell me the truth."

He took a moment to think about it, remembering the fantasies of the perfect wife and family he'd created as a teenager—sure enough, his dream wife had always been a homemaker. Somehow, Vicki had picked up on something he'd shoved to the back of his consciousness. "It is nice having you at home, but only if you're content to be here. I want you to be happy, whatever that takes."

"Really?"

"Really. See? No big problem." He was trying very hard to be encouraging, though he worried that the more involved she grew with her new job, the less time she'd have for him and their child. The voice of the boy inside him, the one who'd been pushed to the periphery of everyone's life, wasn't quite as easy to silence as he'd believed.

"You know, for the first time in a long, long while, I'm starting to feel good about myself, like I'm worth something," Vicki said, leaning forward with her elbows on her knees.

He frowned and copied her gesture, looking at the silhouette of her face. "You're worth everything to me."

She smiled but it was bittersweet. "Until a few days ago, I thought I was an afterthought in your life." When he would have spoken, she stopped him with one finger against his lips. "I'm not blaming you. This has to do with how I see myself, not how you see me."

"How do you see yourself?" he asked, aware that she'd taken his accusations during their blowup on Sunday night to heart. Without any prompting on his part, she was telling him her secrets.

"I'm not proud of who I am and I want to be. I want to be a woman with goals, ambitions, dreams." Her eyes held such determination when she turned to him that he was stunned. "I want to live, Caleb. I want to look back on my life without regrets."

His gut tightened. "Why didn't you ever say anything before?"

"I was fine with the situation at first." She reached out and tangled the fingers of one of her hands with his, giving him a little peace. "It was kind of nice to be taken care of. No one had ever done that for me without making me feel like a burden."

"You were never that." To him, she was a gift, a creature of grace who'd found him to her liking.

"I know. That was what was so seductive. I let myself believe that it was okay to be looked after, to merely exist." Her fingers squeezed his. "I should've been looking after you, too—you needed the care as much as I did."

"How could you have known about Max?" Caleb scowled. "I was too bloody stubborn to talk."

"Don't you see, even if Max had been the perfect father, as your wife, I should've been fulfilling your needs, whatever they were. But I wasn't. I was letting you do all the work while I sat back." She tried out a smile. "I think I'm getting better at that part of it."

"You're perfect." He repeated her statement about him.

"But I can't build my whole sense of self around you. That's not healthy. It would suffocate you and negate my own strengths. I want to achieve things in life on my own. I want to find passion for something like you have for the firm."

"What about us? Not you or me, but what we are together?" He raised their clasped hands and kissed her knuckles. "We burn up together."

Her cheeks flushed. "Yes, we do. And I wouldn't change that for the world."

"But you need something else." Something he couldn't give her. His ego was taking a battering. He would never stop her doing what she wanted, but he couldn't understand why being his wife and the mother of his child wasn't enough.

"It's the same reason you go to work every day," she whispered. "You're living your dream. That's all I want—a dream of my own."

Caleb felt his heart break. He'd been focusing on the effect of her actions on him, when he should have been listening to what she'd been trying to say almost since the moment they'd gotten back together. His Vicki hadn't ever been given a chance to find out what her dreams were, much less whether they lay in being a wife and mother or something else entirely. What right did he have to deny her the same joy he'd found chasing his own?

"Then go out and find it." She could have had no idea what it took for him to say those words. After the life he'd lived, he was possessive beyond reason. She was his, the only person who'd ever been his. Except she never really had been. That woman had been a shadow of the one he was now beginning to know.

This new woman he was learning layer by layer would have to decide whether or not she wanted to belong to him, body and soul. And if she decided to give her passion to something else, leaving him the dregs? A good man, an unselfish man, would have let her embrace that new passion without hindrance. But Caleb found that where his wife was concerned, he wasn't a good man. He was damn selfish. Though he'd let her chase her dreams, he'd fight for her passion.

He'd fight to be her dream.

The next day, Vicki was alone in the house when she got a call from her grandmother. Ada wanted to know why she hadn't seen Caleb and Vicki for dinner since they'd begun living together again.

"We've been very busy," Vicki said, a sick feeling in the pit of her stomach.

"I know he's a busy man but you could've made the time." Ada knew precisely what to say to hurt the most.

"I've started a new job."

Ada laughed. "What? Some charity thing? Really, Victoria, I've been doing that all my life."

Vicki didn't want to sully her hopes by putting them out for Ada's examination. "I know."

"So you'll come to dinner tonight at seven. I'll have the cook make something Italian. I know Caleb likes Italian." Without another word, she hung up.

Vicki groaned and dropped her head into her hands. Why had she let her grandmother bully her like that? She wasn't some weakling. She'd proven that again and again in the past few days. But it was as if the years of her life that she'd lived under Ada's control had scarred her permanently. When her grandmother had started browbeating her, she'd withdrawn into the protective shell she'd thought she'd never need again.

Picking up the phone, she called Caleb and told him what had happened. "I'm sorry, I just couldn't say no." She winced at how pathetic she sounded. "I did the hermit crab routine." Even though she could now see her coping tactic for what it was, it was hard to break out of the instinctive reaction.

To her surprise, he chuckled. "As long as you don't do it with me, you're allowed the occasional relapse."

"I feel like such a pushover."

"Don't take it so hard, honey. Both of us have our weak spots. Who says we have to deal with them alone? You keep Lara at bay. I'll take care of Queen Ada."

His willingness to accept her help made her feel better. "Do you want to go?"

"Might as well. Otherwise she'll keep hounding you. Tell you what, I'll charm the old bat into donating a ton to Heart."

She burst out laughing. "I can't believe you said that."

"I thought I was being nice. Then again, you're the only one I'm ever nice to." His chuckle was sinful enough to curl her toes. "I won't have time to change so she'll have to take me as I am."

She bit her lip, then pushed on bravely. "You're very sexy as you are."

A short silence. "You can't say things like that to me when I'm in the middle of drafting a memo. I think I just misspelled the client's name." His voice was husky, holding echoes of the pleasure they'd found in each other's arms the night before.

"Come home for lunch," she whispered, scandalized at herself. Who was this woman enticing her husband so boldly?

Caleb groaned. "I have a meeting way out in the suburbs at one o'clock."

Disappointment nipped her flaring sensuality in the bud. "I'll see you around six-thirty, then?"

"Bye, sweetheart."

When the bell rang a little before twelve, she didn't think anything of it. Walking to the door, she opened it, expecting a deliveryman, and gasped in surprise as Caleb pushed inside. "I have twenty minutes before I have to leave for the meeting." He kicked the door shut and kissed her. Hard.

Moaning into his mouth, she didn't protest when his fingers went to the top of her sweatpants. Her body had gone from cool to blazing hot in the space of two seconds. He pushed down her panties at the same time as her sweatpants and broke the kiss barely long enough to bend down and whip the garments off her feet.

Rising, he ran his hands up the backs of her thighs to her buttocks. She wrapped her arms and legs tightly around him as he lifted her and pressed her against the wall. When he didn't move fast enough for her, she grabbed his face and brought his mouth to hers for a kiss, so hungry for him that she wanted to scream. There was no room for fear or inhibition. Everything was happening too fast. She bit at his lower lip and felt him jerk.

His hand slipped over her stomach and then his fingers were stroking her with raw intimacy. Hard and fast, it was propelling her over the edge. When he drove two fingers deep inside her, she screamed, her hands clenching on his shoulders. "Caleb!"

His fingers left her and, a second later, she felt the blunt tip of his erection pushing into her. "You're so hot, sweetheart. So damn tight."

She couldn't speak, her body starting to shudder even

before he was completely inside her. Groaning, he entered her fully. That was all it took. She orgasmed so violently that she saw stars. With a shout, he began to rock in and out of her, his movements powerful and strong. But a part of her was aware that he held her carefully even in his passion, never letting her slam into the wall. And then even that measure of thought was lost and she became a creature of sensation and pleasure.

When she opened her eyes, she found Caleb slumped against her with his head buried in the crook of her neck. Hot bursts of air hit her skin as he breathed in ragged gasps. Under her fingers, the material of his business shirt was damp and wrinkled, the heat of his body almost burning. Unclenching her hands, she stroked her hand up into his hair.

He nuzzled at her and kissed the beat of her pulse before raising his head. When their gazes met, she saw such joy that she was stunned. Smiling, she leaned forward and rubbed her nose against his in a silly affectionate gesture. He chuckled, his hands sliding to hold the backs of her thighs.

"You have—" she glanced at the hall clock "—twelve minutes left to shower and eat." She couldn't stop stroking his body, his face. He was so dear to her and at last he was treating her like his wife, his woman, one who could take everything he had to give.

All this time she'd concentrated on the pain that would come if she ventured outside her protective walls. Today she'd been shown the flip side—endless pleasure and the most incredible happiness.

He groaned and started to pull out, releasing her legs as he did so. When they were finally extricated, he kissed her and said, "Shower?"

Her eyes went wide. "I'll make you late." But she put her hand in his and let him lead her to the bathroom off their bedroom.

Once there, he tugged off her sweater and unclipped her bra while she worked feverishly to pull off his tie and undo the buttons on his shirt. It took them maybe a minute to get naked and under the shower, the cool spray a crisp relief to their overheated bodies.

"Eleven minutes." Caleb picked up the soap.

Before he could touch her with it, she took it from him. "You're the one who needs to hurry." She lathered up her hands and returned the soap. "I'll do your back." She forced herself not to linger over her self-appointed task, though she wanted to luxuriate. This was not how she'd thought her fantasy would play out but it worked for her. "Done."

Instead of turning off the water, Caleb looked at the waterproof watch strapped to his wrist. "Eight minutes. I have time." And then he started to torture her.

She wondered how she could possibly want him again after the heat that had singed her in the hallway. His hands, soapy and slick, were everywhere. When they slipped between her thighs to bring her effortlessly to her second orgasm in under twenty minutes, she felt her legs turn to jelly.

"Done," he rasped as she collapsed in his arms, the water pounding at them. "Six minutes."

She made herself turn off the shower with sheer strength of will and got out. Rubbing herself haphazardly with a towel, she grabbed the robe at the back of the door. "I'm going to warm up something for you to eat."

He tried to catch her as she whipped out but she laughed and escaped him. The last thing she saw as she ran from the room was the sight of his glorious body shiny with clear droplets of water, his hair tangled and wet.

Three minutes later, he walked into the kitchen dressed in a dark suit, white shirt and blue tie almost identical to what he'd been wearing earlier. His grin was wicked. "If I return to the office looking too different, people might wonder what I've been up to."

She felt her cheeks heat up. "Eat. It's nothing special but it'll fill you up."

He came around the counter and stood beside her, eating quickly as she found an insulated travel mug and filled it with hot coffee, screwing the lid closed. "For the road." She put it in his hand as he finished the meal in record time.

They were at the door five seconds after the twenty minutes had passed. Unable to resist, she reached up, wrapped her arms around his neck and kissed the life out of him. When she drew back, red streaked his cheekbones and there was a spark in his eyes she'd never before seen. Her Caleb was starting to come home to her in more ways than one.

"Hold that thought," he whispered, backing out the door.

"I'll be waiting." She watched him until he'd pulled out of the driveway. A huge grin creased her face as she closed the door. She couldn't believe what she'd just done. Not only had she had the fastest, most furious sex with her husband, she'd showered with him. Two fantasies taken care of in twenty minutes. Not bad. Not bad at all.

She was waiting for Caleb to pick her up for the ride to Ada's when he called. "I'm sorry, sweetheart. I've got to stay at the office."

Disappointment deflated the lingering joy from their lovemaking. "I'll go alone, then."

"No, you won't. I keep my promises." His voice was caressing. "I got us off the hook. We're not due at Ada's until Sunday, now. Together."

A slow smile whispered across her face. "How did you manage that?"

"By lying creatively," he said, unrepentant. "I'll try to be home by nine."

"See you then." She hung up the phone feeling very good about her marriage. Not only was Caleb learning to let go of work a little, he was starting to learn *her.* She hadn't missed the fact that he was working late once again. But he'd taken off Monday to be with her, so he was probably playing catch-up.

She understood what his work demanded of him at times. That was part of the reason she wanted something of her own. Aside from giving her a sense of pride, it would provide her with something to hold on to when Caleb's devotion to his work pushed her aside.

And if, deep down, there was a niggling voice worrying that maybe her husband wasn't busy with work at all but something, *someone,* else, she buried it under so many layers of denial that she managed to convince herself it had ceased to exist.

On Friday night, Vicki accepted that she'd made a colossal mistake. It was 3:00 a.m. and she'd just heard the sound of Caleb's car through the autumn rain. He'd worked late every single day since their wild lovemaking in the hallway, apparently taking her calm acceptance of that first late night as a free pass to go back to his workaholic ways.

She'd finished several memos for Heart during the time that she'd waited up for him. Now, she walked into the kitchen, poured coffee into two cups and carried it into the living room. The location was a deliberate choice on her part. Their new and vibrant sensual connection had had an unexpected side effect. Caleb was a very sexual man and she'd been starving for him for too long to ever deny him. As a result, too many of their problems were being buried under the blazing fire of their lovemaking.

"Vicki?" he called out as he walked through the back door, obviously having seen the light.

"In here." Shifting several magazines to the side of the coffee table, she wondered how she was going to broach the subject without creating a huge fight. Sounding like a nag was the last thing she wanted to do but this was important, both for her and for their child. As she'd told Caleb, she refused to have their baby feel like an unwelcome obligation.

However, her priorities changed the second he walked in. She knew something was terribly wrong. It wasn't because his suit was wet from the rain or that his hair looked wildly tumbled as if he'd been running his fingers through it. It was the bleak look in his eyes. The only time she'd seen him look that way was the night he'd inadvertently revealed his pain at the way she'd kicked him out of their home.

"What's happened?" She walked over to help him with his coat.

He let her hang it up before collapsing on the couch. She sat down next to him, worried. "Caleb, honey?"

"I'm just tired." He stared at the wall opposite the sofa but she knew he wasn't seeing the painting hanging there.

"No," she said, cupping his jaw with one hand and turning him to face her. "You don't get to do that anymore."

"Do what?" He raised his hand to hers but didn't pull her away.

"Keep secrets that cause you pain." She shook her head in reproval.

"You don't need to be stressed right now. I don't want anything to hurt you."

His tenderness broke her heart. How could she not keep sinking deeper in her feelings for him? "You know what hurts me the most? Being shut out of your life. Don't do that to me, Caleb. Not again." Her voice trembled with the intensity of her emotions.

Looking at her with eyes clouded by unknown demons, he opened his arms. She tucked her body against his and held him. Would he speak to her? Would he take the next step in this new relationship they were building? A relationship of equals, where she took as much responsibility for him as he'd always taken for her.

"Two days ago," he began to explain, "a huge deal we've been working on for almost a year started to come apart at the seams."

"What happened?"

"Maxwell is our client. Horrocks the buyer. We were almost to the signing stage when Horrocks discovered a major discrepancy in the financial reports provided by Maxwell during due diligence."

She'd read enough business journals to appreciate the scale of the problem. "Horrocks is refusing to sign?"

"More than that, they're accusing Maxwell of deliberate subterfuge."

Vicki knew that Caleb was an absolute perfectionist in his work. He would never do anything underhanded. "Did someone on the Maxwell side let you down?"

"Not deliberately. It was basically a massive cock-up

on the part of their chief financial officer and his staff." He sighed and dropped his chin onto her hair. "Did you see the paper today?"

"No, I didn't have time." Warned by his tone, she walked over to the side table where she'd put the paper after it had been delivered and carried it back to him.

Caleb took it from her and waited until she was sitting with him again before opening it to the front page of the business section. What he saw still made his stomach churn. "Respected Law Firm Fumbles Billion-Dollar Buyout," he read out, feeling his dreams collapse.

A gentle hand touched his shoulder. "You know you didn't fumble it. Is the deal still alive? Have you got something to work with?"

He dropped the paper onto a cushion. "Barely. If we can't get Horrocks to agree to give Maxwell time to clear up this issue, it really will gurgle down the drain."

"The fault was Maxwell's, not yours."

"No. It was ours. Maxwell is our client and we should've picked up this problem." He refused to go easy on himself.

Victoria slapped his shoulder, making him look down at her scowling face. "You're a lawyer, not an accountant. These are financial problems."

"Callaghan & Associates was in charge of the overall deal from the Maxwell side. We were paid to ensure *everything* went smoothly." Taking her hand from his shoulder, he kissed the tips of her fingers. "If we don't rescue this deal, the firm will begin to hemorrhage clients. The end."

Her eyes flared. "If it comes to that, *we* start over, even if that means I have to be your secretary." She smiled. "No regrets."

A weight lifted off his chest. A small part of him had worried that she'd welcome the closure of a firm she saw as a rival for his attention. "No regrets?"

"Never."

He thanked God for her. One of his associates was already feeling the pressure from his socialite wife—she wanted assurance that she'd be kept in the style to which she'd become accustomed.

Vicki stroked the line of his jaw. "I have every faith in you. You'll succeed. Can I do anything to help?"

"Thanks, honey, but unless you can convince my clients not to cut and run before we fix this, it's up to me and the team."

"Hmm." Vicki tapped her mouth with one finger. "I have an idea."

"Should I be worried? The last time you had an idea, I spent two months living in a hotel."

The words were out of Vicki's mouth almost before she'd thought them. "Yes well, I had a little help in that from you." She knew it was the worst possible time to bring this up but it was out of her control—some switch in her had inadvertently been thrown by his flip comment.

"I wasn't exactly a prize husband, huh?" He grimaced. "But we're doing okay."

"Are we really?" Why was she doing this now? she thought, horrified at the destruction she was about to instigate. She'd thought she'd put this issue in the past where it belonged but that had obviously been a huge lie, a final remnant of the self-protective shell she was so used to living in. "We promised no more secrets and yet…"

"You think there's something else we need to clear up?" There was nothing but concern in his voice.

"We've never talked about Miranda." The words fell

like grenades between them. At the same time, a sweeping sense of relief washed over her. Until she'd spoken, she hadn't realized the pressure that had built up inside of her.

"Miranda? What the hell does she have to do with anything?"

The complete lack of understanding on his face made a sick feeling crawl through her stomach, curdling the relief. Either Caleb was flat-out lying to her, or she'd made a terrible mistake. And Caleb wasn't a man for subtleties—there was no way he could have counterfeited his confusion.

Suddenly, comprehension swept across his expression. "Goddamn it, Vicki!" He thrust his hands through his hair. "I can't believe what I'm seeing on your face. Say the damn words."

It was too late to back away. Far too late. "I knew our marriage was in trouble for a long time," she said, "but the reason I decided to ask for a divorce was because I thought you were having an affair with Miranda." It had been the proverbial straw that had broken the camel's back…broken *her.* Infidelity was the one thing she couldn't take, perhaps because of the guilt she'd always carried on her mother's behalf.

His eyes grew hard with anger. "Why?"

She knew he deserved answers. "You were always at the office late and when I called, she'd answer and say you couldn't come to the phone."

"That was enough to convict me?" His tone was clipped and he didn't touch her.

She wondered if, after everything they'd done to repair their marriage, she was going to lose him because of her own stupidity. The idea of never being able to hear his laughter felt like a knife to the soul.

Pushing back the fear, she looked straight into his eyes. She had to confront this head-on. She was no longer that woman who'd tried to bury her pain and keep going with a marriage she'd believed had been betrayed...without once *asking* Caleb if he'd done what she'd judged him guilty of.

"No. I mean it made me suspicious—we both know I wasn't the most confident of women then."

"Vicki," Caleb began, a frown on his face.

"Let me finish," she begged. "I can't do this twice."

"Talk." When he raised his arm and slid it along the back of the sofa, his fingers touching her nape, the relief she felt was almost crushing. Caleb's touch was her anchor when everything else spun out of control.

"Then you went on that trip to Wellington four months ago and she went with you. Remember?"

"Yes." Of course Caleb remembered. In nearly five years of marriage, it had been the first time he'd left his wife for more than a week and he'd ached for her every moment. But she hadn't cared enough about their relationship to make the first move for once and call him. Hurt more than he would have thought possible, believing that their marriage had come to the worst place it possibly could be, he hadn't contacted her, either.

"I missed you so." Vicki's eyes were bright blue with emotion. "I couldn't sleep without you there beside me."

All his conclusions about the past came to a screeching halt.

"That first night you were gone, I waited and waited for you to call like you always did. When you didn't, I finally picked up the phone at around 3:00 a.m. I tried your cell phone first but you must've turned it off, so I called your hotel room instead." Her hands fisted against him. "*She* answered!"

Those fists hit his shoulders, as if the emotion inside

her had become too much to bear. "She said you were out on the balcony but she could get you if I wanted. The way she spoke…how was I supposed to think anything else? We'd had that fight and you'd been so angry—angry enough to do something hurtful."

Before he could say anything in his defense, she took a jerky breath and hit him with words of such raw emotion, he could hardly believe it was his restrained, elegant Victoria in his arms.

"Then you came back and you wouldn't touch me! You didn't want me at all and I thought she'd given you what I couldn't. What was she doing in your room, Caleb? Why was she answering *your* phone in the middle of the night?" Her hands pushed against his chest, distancing her body from his.

He'd never seen her this way—pure fury, pure rage. "We swapped rooms," he said, wondering if she'd believe him.

"What?" Her face was a study in confusion. "Why?"

"The hotel made a mistake with the booking. I was given the smoking room and Miranda the non-smoking one." He paused, remembering the events of that week. "Unless they didn't make a mistake… She couldn't have planned it?" After his fight with Vicki, he'd been in one hell of a mood during the flight to Wellington. Miranda hadn't said a word about his temper, had instead been full of concern.

Now that he thought about it, he could see what he'd missed at the time—the woman had been offering much more than sympathy. It must have burned her when he hadn't responded to her overtures. He could well imagine her pursuing him by attempting to wreck his marriage.

Vicki took another shuddering breath. "Didn't the desk staff know? They're the ones who transferred my call."

"We checked in very late at night. Remember, we took the last flight. When we discovered the mistake, we just swapped rooms and Miranda said she'd deal with the desk in the morning." His whole body thrummed with tension.

"Oh, God." Vicki swallowed and shoved her hands in her hair, face pale and drawn. "But you didn't want me. You didn't touch me for a week! And you *always* touched me before. No matter what, you always touched me!"

"I was hurting." If Vicki was being honest with her pain, he could do no less. "I'd wanted my wife to care enough about me to contact me, to make up for that fight. But as far as I knew, you hadn't bothered."

"She was incredibly convincing. If you'd heard her…" Vicki's voice was a whisper now. "It hurt me so much that you might've been with another woman. It broke my heart."

He stared at her, his certainties long gone. "I've never cheated on you and I never will." Even the fact that he'd once angrily considered such a thing had caused him endless guilt. He could never take that step and live with himself. *Never.* "Fidelity is the only weapon I had to fight the shame Max convinced me was my heritage. It's something I'm incapable of betraying. Do you believe me?"

The blunt question made her tremble. "Yes. Oh, God, *yes.*" When she raised her head, there was such need in her gaze that he was lost. "I'm so sorry, Caleb. I should've talked to you, not just…"

He *was* angry at her for her lack of trust but not enough to relish her suffering. And it hadn't been all her doing. "I remember what I was like after I got back. No wonder you didn't want to bring up the subject. And you were right about one thing."

"What?"

"The reason I have a new secretary is because Miranda hit on me heavily a few days after you and I separated." It had enraged him that anyone would dare question his loyalty to his marriage, to his wife. He'd been brutal in his rejection of Miranda. "When she realized I'd rather slit my own throat than take her up on the offer, she resigned, and I brushed it off as a lapse in judgment on her part. If I'd known what she'd done in Wellington…"

Vicki let out a short, choked scream. "I can't believe I almost killed myself worrying about something that wasn't true! Over four months I let that thing fester inside me, telling myself I could get past it, that I could accept it for the sake of our child. And all that time, I *knew* I'd never be able to forgive and forget."

"I guess that's your punishment. And it's over," he said, meaning it. He wasn't going to let Miranda's lies push him into throwing away this marriage they'd rebuilt with their hearts and their souls. And nothing he could do would equal the torment Vicki had put herself through.

Not only that, but the fact that she'd spoken to him about her worries instead of continuing to let them grow, was in itself a sign of the deepest trust. "Cheating is the one thing you never have to worry about with me, honey. Between you and the firm, when would I have the time?" He wanted to make her laugh, wanted to ease the ache.

Instead, she wrapped her arms tightly around his neck and crawled into his lap. "We'll save your firm, Caleb. Nobody's going to take it from you. *I promise.*"

Struck by the fierceness of the declaration, he crushed her to him. Yet, even as he held her, he knew that there was something he wasn't hearing. And this time, he didn't even know what question to ask to find out the hidden truth.

* * *

Two days and hours of hard work on both their parts later, Caleb found himself presiding over a dinner party involving nine of his biggest clients and their spouses. Kent Jacobs and his fiancée—another woman who'd stuck by her man—were also present.

Midway through the meal, when everyone seemed to be relaxed and at ease, an older client leaned across and said, "Caleb, you've been my first choice for eight years, since before you had your own firm. I won't run scared but neither will I let my company sink with you.

"We simply can't afford to be linked with a firm that has an image of incompetence if you'll forgive my bluntness. *I* know you're the best but I have to answer to shareholders who get their information from the media."

Pensive silence descended on the table, but Caleb was glad for the opportunity to lay things out in the open. He took a deep breath, caught Vicki's eye and began to speak. Here went nothing.

No regrets.

"We have every confidence we can rescue this deal. All we ask is that you don't precipitate a crisis in the firm by withdrawing your files prematurely." It was a bold request but none of these people liked dancing around hard facts. "If the deal crumbles, we'll cooperate fully in transferring files to your new attorneys. Just hold off your decision for two weeks."

The man who'd originally spoken nodded. Like the others around this table, he was used to making quick decisions. "I'm willing to do that. You're the best—I don't want to lose you if there's a chance you can come out on top."

One by one, after a few more probing questions, every one of his clients agreed. They had two weeks' grace.

* * *

In bed that night, Caleb hugged Victoria. "Breathing room."

"I'm with you all the way."

"I know." That knowledge gave him more drive and determination than anything else. "The next two weeks will be tough."

"Tougher than our separation?"

"Nothing could be as tough as that." That quickly, everything was put into perspective. "What's the worst that could happen? The deal falls apart and my firm goes down the toilet along with my reputation."

Vicki's eyes filled with laughter at his mournful tone. "And?"

"And we start over again." The vise around his chest loosened. "We won't be destitute. I've got enough saved in investments to last us a long while."

"I could keep you," she suggested, kissing his neck. "I still have that money from the trust fund that came to me on my twenty-first birthday. Plus, I'll be getting paid soon."

"The life of a kept man," he murmured. "Might have something going for it."

Her teeth scraped his jaw. "You'd go nuts within the first hour." There was a chuckle in her words, affection in the way she touched him.

"Yup. But I can dream." He turned his head to capture her wandering lips with his own.

The kiss held his devotion to her. It was tender and beautiful and this side of ravenous. When they parted, her eyes were slumberous but her lips didn't smile. "Caleb, we're okay, aren't we?"

He immediately knew what she was referring to. "We're

stronger than ever. All you did was prove you can act as much a fool as me."

She made a face. "Guilty as charged. I won't ever doubt you again."

"I know." And he did. Because he hadn't lied—their marriage had only become stronger after she'd trusted him enough to bring up the painful subject. "Good night, baby."

"Good night, Caleb," she whispered, placing her head against his chest, her hand over his heart.

Content, he slept.

Twelve

For the next ten days, sleep was an elusive commodity. Caleb and his entire team worked like men and women possessed. And through it all, Victoria was there, the anchor in his life that let him forge ahead without destroying himself with worry.

No regrets.

During the third day, she turned up with muffins for everyone. It gave his overworked staff a cheerful moment and considerably boosted morale. For the thousandth time, Caleb thanked God for her.

Pulling her into his office, he held her tight. "How was your day?"

"Busy. I think I've lined up a corporate sponsor for the charity concert I'm organizing, but it's tricky at the moment. The good news is that the radio interviews are set to go." Her hand stroked his back. "You?"

"We're doing everything we can but so far, nothing concrete." He adored her for helping him fight for his dream even as she chased her own. "Heart would be crazy to let you go."

"Thanks for the vote of confidence." Her smile turned a little wicked. "And thanks for setting up this crisis as an excuse to not keep our dinner appointment with Ada."

Her words made him laugh. "I did it all for you."

"I know." A more solemn look came over her face. "Can I lend a hand here in any way?"

He kissed her. "Go home and rest. I need to know that you and the baby are okay."

"We're fine. We're more than fine."

"In that case, you're welcome to keep feeding us. I think Kent was making noises about cinnamon rolls."

Their shared laughter filled the air.

Vicki left Caleb's office building with a smile. It lasted until she answered her cell phone ten minutes later. The number was unfamiliar but the voice wasn't.

"Hello, Vicki."

"Mother." Vicki moved to stand with her back to a wall. She'd never really expected her mother to fly to New Zealand to see her. Danica wasn't exactly the most reliable of women. "Are you in Auckland?"

"I've just left the airport. Can you spare time for coffee with me tomorrow, say around eleven?"

Vicki's mind was in turmoil, her thoughts skittering. "Sure."

"Why don't you meet me at that nice little coffee shop we went to last year?"

"That sounds fine."

Minutes later, Vicki was still standing on the street. She wanted to run to Caleb, let him hold her and ask him to make it all right. Nobody, not even Ada, could destroy her composure the way Danica could. Like a whirlwind, she'd sweep into Vicki's life once a year or so and leave emotional devastation behind.

Danica wasn't a bad person, but simply so self-involved that she had no time to be a mother, no time to listen to her daughter's needs. During her last visit, Vicki would have done anything to have her mother's advice on how to fix the fissures in her marriage. But Danica had been interested only in talking about her trip to Paris.

"Excuse me, miss."

She turned, startled. The elderly man who'd spoken tipped an imaginary hat toward her and started to read the signboard she'd been blocking. The interruption was precisely what she'd needed to snap her out of her frozen state.

She walked to her car. This was her problem and she'd deal with it. No more hiding, either behind her own walls, or behind Caleb's strength. If she still couldn't handle Danica, then everything she'd said to Caleb about becoming her own woman was a lie. And she didn't want it to be.

Caleb came home well after midnight. Vicki was asleep so he tried not to wake her as he got ready for bed. In the glow of the single bedside light he'd turned on, she looked so beautiful that he stood watching her for a long moment.

God, he could barely believe she was his. Her skin bloomed with health, so soft and silky that sometimes he was afraid of bruising her with his touch. Dressed in her favorite old pj's, she was curled up on her side, legs drawn to her chest. He wanted nothing more than to hold her through the night. Sliding in beside her, he turned off the light and pulled her into his embrace.

"Caleb?" she murmured, snuggling sleepily into him.

"Go back to sleep, honey." He pressed a kiss to the curve of her neck and then lay down to rest, feeling blessed.

No matter what happened with his business, he would always have Victoria. His wife's commitment to him was so powerful, he knew it would never falter. She might not love him the way he needed to be loved, but she'd never again leave him. When a man had that kind of loyalty behind him, failure wasn't something to be terrified of.

"No regrets," he whispered as the night claimed him.

Mid-morning the next day, Vicki stared at the screen of her cell phone, fighting the urge to call Caleb. He didn't need to be burdened with her problem. Not now. But despite everything she'd tried to convince herself, she was scared she wouldn't be able to handle Danica. She'd almost said something to Caleb as he'd left for work. What had stopped her then was the same thing that stopped her now—her own need to prove that she was strong enough to face up to the brutal reality of her childhood.

Closing the phone, she returned it to her purse and picked up her coffee to take a sip. As she did so, she realized something important. Though she'd come to meet Danica on her own, she was no longer alone as she'd been for most of her life. Caleb's faith in her was an invisible presence by her side.

A flash of red at the door of the café caught her attention. Putting down her cup, she watched the beautiful blonde walk over. Though she was well into her fifties, there was nothing old about Danica Wentworth née Striker. Her hair was a gold-streaked mane that tumbled around her shoulders, her body curved and toned and her makeup flawless. In a simple wraparound dress that bared her arms and showed off her cleavage, she was sexy enough to make heads turn.

Danica stopped by Vicki's table. "Victoria, darling." The scent of her perfume was painfully familiar, awakening memories Vicki didn't want to remember.

She stood and dutifully pecked Danica on the cheek. "Hello, Mother." As she sat back down, Danica folded herself into the chair opposite, her every move confident and sensual. Vicki felt dull by comparison, a swallow next to a bird of paradise.

"That blue looks good on you, darling." Danica waved at the sky-blue cardigan Vicki had teamed with her favorite jeans. She liked the softness of the cashmere against her skin but most of all, she liked how Caleb was tempted into stroking her whenever she wore this fabric.

"Aren't you cold?" she asked Danica.

Her mother laughed. "I'm hot-blooded. Did you order me a coffee?"

"Flat white, no sugar."

"Perfect."

Danica's coffee arrived moments later and she paused to send a blinding smile the waiter's way before taking a sip. "Um, wonderful, though I must admit I miss the coffee I get back home."

"How is Italy?" That was where Danica had gone after meeting Carlo Belladucci and it was a place to which Vicki had never been invited.

Danica's smiling face suddenly sombered. Putting down her cup, she reached across the table and placed her hand over Vicki's. Vicki was so surprised that she didn't react. "I came to say I'm sorry."

"For what?"

"For everything—for leaving you to Ada, for deciding to chase my love for Carlo instead of looking after my daughter, for never being there for you." Danica's blue eyes, so like Vicki's own, filled with a plea for under-standing. "Forgive me."

Vicki knew it meant nothing. It hadn't meant anything the last few times Danica had been overcome by guilt. And it didn't mean anything today. It never would. Danica was a fickle, beautiful butterfly. That she'd stuck with Carlo this long was a testament to her love for the man. Danica had managed to turn into a faithful lover but she'd never be maternal.

The amazing thing was, that lack in Danica no longer cut Vicki's heart to pieces. It was a startling insight but more than welcome. "There's nothing to forgive," she said gently, aware of the life growing inside of her. Without her conscious knowledge, Caleb and her baby had given her the emotional strength to withstand Danica's butterfly persona, dramatically shifting her priorities from the shadowed past to a sparkling future.

"My therapist says I can't get closure until I let you re-lease your anger at me."

Putting her hand over her mother's and clasping that slender hand in her own, she smiled. "Tell him or her that I'm not angry at you." Not anymore. "I'm happy that you're happy, Mother. You are, aren't you?"

"Oh yes." Danica pulled her hand away. "What about you, darling? How's your gorgeous husband?"

"I'm wonderful and so is Caleb." She smiled, able to share the news with Danica now without any bitterness. "We're going to have a baby."

Danica gave an excited shriek that made the whole café look at them but her mother had never cared about the world's opinion. "Oh, darling. How exciting! Good God, that means I'll be a grandmother!"

"You'll be the crazily beautiful grandmother who

comes in and sweeps my child off her feet." Vicki knew that to be the absolute truth. Free with gifts and laughter, Danica would fill a child's life with infectious joy. Just so long as no commitment beyond periodic visits was required. "You'll be adored."

Danica seemed to like that idea. As she happily burbled away about everything from the designer baby clothes she was going to buy to her adventures in Europe, Vicki felt another understanding dawn in her mind. Danica, she realized, didn't *want* to be married or tied down in any way. What Ada had held as a threat over Vicki's head was for Danica a perfect life. Her mother was no one's mistress but her own.

Something in Vicki healed completely at that thought and she saw Ada for the pitiful woman she was. Her grandmother had based her life on a thousand lies, big and small. She was no one to be scared of. Vicki knew with absolute certainty that never again would Ada have the power to force her back into her shell.

An hour later, she said goodbye to her mother outside the café and they went their separate ways.

Vicki decided to walk over and browse in a nearby lingerie store, her mind at peace. It was a wonderful change from all those times when Danica's appearances had left her feeling as if she were four years old again and watching her mother wave goodbye from a limousine as she headed off to a new life.

Vicki's fingers touched the lacy edge of a moss-green camisole and she paused. It was attractive but definitely an extravagance.

I like seeing you in satin and lace.

The memory of the unexpected words made her

decision for her. She picked up the camisole. Pretty and feminine, she knew it would make her feel special.

The way Caleb did.

Standing there with the plastic hanger in one hand, Vicki realized that she loved Caleb more than she'd ever imagined. The feeling was primitive and visceral, demanding everything she had. *This* was why she'd been able to truly forgive her mother, because she knew Danica had never felt anything like it and never would.

Her mother enjoyed life, lived and laughed, but she'd never given her heart and soul to anyone or anything. Not to her child, not to her safely married lover, not to her work. Vicki had fallen helplessly in love with Caleb and as helplessly in love with their unborn child.

She'd tried to find a passion, a dream, in an attempt to fight the knowledge that *Caleb* was her dream. It had been her way of coping with the fact that work was his life. No more, she thought. Just because he couldn't return her feelings didn't mean he didn't deserve to know how she felt.

Perhaps that made her a fool. Then again, perhaps it made her the luckiest woman alive. Smiling through eyes gone watery, she picked up the lace-edged panties that matched the camisole and took them to the counter.

That night, Caleb managed to make it home by eight. Vicki was outside chatting to their neighbor, Bill, and he joined her for a few minutes before they headed in out of the chill air.

"How are things?" she asked.

"There might be a light at the end of the tunnel." Holding the door open for her, he let her take his briefcase and put it next to a nearby table. "Something smells good."

"I made pasta. And I ate a ton of it." She scrunched up

her face. "I'm going to be huge by the time she decides it's time to come out."

Chuckling, he followed her into the living room. "I guess I'll have to survive on what's left over."

"Don't worry. I've learned my lesson by now. I make twice as much as I used to."

As they passed the coffee table, he glanced down to see an open photo album. "What were you doing with this?" He remembered it from soon after they'd married, when Ada had presented it to them. It was a professionally collated piece of work that chronicled Vicki's life from birth to marriage.

"Let me put the pasta on to heat first. Wait here—I'll be back in a second."

Taking her at her word, he shed his jacket, loosened his tie and sat with the album in his lap. He knew Vicki didn't care for it, much preferring the ones she'd started after their wedding. Once, he'd asked her why she didn't like the pictures of her childhood and she'd answered, "They make me feel abandoned."

It had taken him a night of leafing through those pages alone to understand. There were very few photos of Vicki with either parent after she turned four. He'd counted perhaps eight in all and three had been studio shots taken to commemorate her father's remarriage. Eight photos for fifteen years of life. She had a right to feel abandoned.

At least Max and Carmen hadn't thrown him aside until he was old enough to deal with it. And they'd never taunted him with false hope. He couldn't imagine what it must have done to a four-year-old to be left behind by parents who'd professed to love her. It almost allowed him to understand her reluctance to love him heart and soul. In his wife's mind, love led only to a broken heart. How he wished he could undo the lessons of her childhood.

At that moment, Vicki walked in with a plate piled high with pasta and a glass of wine in her hands. "You might as well eat while we talk."

He watched her put the food on the coffee table in front of him. "Thanks, honey. Why don't you...oh right."

"What?" She sat and shifted the album from his lap to hers.

"I was going to ask you to join me in a glass of wine." He smiled. "It still gets me in the gut every time I think about you carrying our kid."

"Me, too." Smiling, she leaned over and kissed him on the cheek. "Eat."

"So what were you doing with that thing?" he asked after a few bites.

"I'm letting myself remember."

"Why?"

"Because I need to. I can't just ignore what happened and still be me. I have to accept the fact that I was hurt by the people who were supposed to love me forever." Her clear blue eyes looked into his. "I have to make peace with the past before I can move on to the future."

His heart leapt into his throat at her implied statement but he was so damn proud of her. "You're the bravest woman I know."

She gave him a rueful smile. "You wouldn't have said that if you'd seen me quaking in my boots before I met Mother for coffee today."

Frowning, he put down his fork and tipped up her chin. "Why didn't you tell me? I could've—"

"Hush." She placed a finger on his lips. "We all have things to face up to and Danica was one of mine. I couldn't keep hiding from what she did to me any more than I can hide from these pictures."

The strength he saw on her face was something he'd never expected to see in the girl he'd married. He was awed by her will, by her ability to move beyond the pain her mother had caused her. In this arena, Vicki was proving far more courageous than him. He could identify the need driving his desperation to save the firm, the need to prove himself to Max all over again, but he couldn't overcome it. Not yet. "What did you decide after seeing her?"

She put her head against his side and began to flip the pages again. "I decided that I shouldn't be afraid of feeling, of loving, of giving my everything. It hurts when it's thrown back in your face but eventually, the pain dims and you can breathe again."

He didn't know how to read that statement, didn't dare to hope. Putting an arm around her, he hugged her close. "Nothing you give me will be rejected. Nothing."

To his surprise, she laughed. "What about my divorce application?"

"Except that." He found himself smiling, too.

She turned a page and pointed to a picture of a somber eight-year-old standing by a bicycle. She was dressed perfectly, her almost white blond hair combed to within an inch of its life. "I could've used you back then. I think I'll always need you. Don't ever leave me, Caleb."

Her last words were heartbreakingly quiet and he felt them in the core of his soul. Outside she was smiling and perhaps even laughing, but in her heart, Vicki was crying. Today she'd surrendered her last hopes and accepted that Danica wouldn't ever be able to give her what she needed. Acceptance didn't mean the pain was any less.

"Never," he whispered, his voice husky from the knot of emotion choking his throat. "I wouldn't go when you asked me to. Why would I leave voluntarily?"

Thirteen

Vicki curled in bed, thinking over the words Caleb had said to her as they sat on the couch. Next to her, he was fast asleep. She'd set the alarm to ring in a few hours so he could return to work, but she couldn't sleep.

For the first time in her life, she was with someone who, quite simply, was too damn stubborn to walk away from her. Some women might have found that kind of possessive commitment daunting, but it was exactly what she needed. When she'd tried to divorce Caleb, she'd hoped to garner his attention, but she hadn't understood the depths to which he'd go to keep the promise he'd made to her on their wedding day.

To love, honor and cherish. For always.

The extent of his loyalty humbled her. Her darling Caleb would be her rock, no matter what life threw at them. It was okay to take risks and open her heart and her body fully to him.

After all these years, the four-year-old girl inside her was smiling. She still felt a little bruised but was healed enough to take the next step.

Getting up out of Caleb's arms, she walked quietly to the dresser and pulled out the lingerie she'd bought today. It was time to start showing her husband what he meant to her. He'd done so much for her and yet expected so little in return.

He'd been abandoned the same way she had and needed as much care and tenderness. The difference was, he'd never allow himself to break down as she'd done countless times, never allow himself to cry or ask for tenderness. She could accept that. It was simply the man he was. But it meant she had to read between the lines where his emotional needs were concerned.

A smile curved her lips—these days she was having no trouble reading Caleb, in bed or out…because her husband trusted her. She had every intention of treasuring that gift, starting now. Tonight she'd give him the tenderness he'd never accept in any other context, show him that she was his in every way.

Slipping out of her pj's, she shimmied into the panties and camisole. There, she thought, feeling a mixture of nervousness and joy. That will surprise him when he wakes. She only hoped he'd understand what she was trying to say. Fighting a shiver, she crawled into bed next to Caleb's warm body. He grumbled in his sleep then cuddled her close.

Caleb woke though the alarm hadn't gone off. Staring at the clock, he realized it was an hour before he had to be up. Yawning, he was about to close his eyes when he registered the texture beneath his palm. Satin. Soft and silky and very touchable. He frowned. He'd been tired when he'd gone to bed but he was sure Vicki had been in her pj's. Carefully, he switched on the bedside light.

Vicki was on her back, her head on one of his arms while his other arm lay across her stomach. Raising the one on her stomach, he lifted away the blanket to have a look, and froze.

These were not Vicki's old pj's.

Unable to do anything else, he bared her completely. She complained in her sleep so he started stroking her upper thighs, gentling her as he took in the delectable sight of his wife's body showcased by satin and lace. The panties were cut high on her thighs, the lace edging the legs meeting the lace of the waistband. In sleep, the camisole had rucked up, exposing a strip of skin on her taut stomach that he couldn't help running his finger over.

"Caleb," she moaned, sounding more than half asleep.

He let his eyes wander up and almost begged for mercy. The left strap had fallen half off, exposing the creamy curve of one breast while the other remained primly covered. What did Vicki think she was doing? He was supposed to be concentrating on saving the Maxwell deal, not drowning in a river of hunger.

One hand on her thigh, he leaned over to drop a kiss on the bared skin of her breast. His stubble rubbed across her skin. She made a sleepy sound and one hand rose to tangle in his hair, keeping him where he was. Delighted, he tugged at the fallen strap until her breast popped free completely and he breathed a sigh of appreciation.

Stroking his hand up her body, he took her nipple between his fingertips and plucked at it, teasing her fully awake. She shifted and he moved enough to slide one hair-roughened thigh between her smooth ones. Rubbing his thumb over her nipple, he felt her hand clench in his hair.

"Caleb, what…?"

"These aren't your pj's," he accused, without looking up from his task. He released her nipple from his fingers only to take it between his teeth. She gasped.

"I wanted to…um…" She gasped again as he let go of the nipple, scraping it with his teeth. "*Caleb.*"

"You wanted to what?" he prompted, cupping her breast in his hand.

"To surprise you." The roughness of desire colored her tone.

He pressed a kiss to her breastbone and rose to look at her. "Why?"

She blushed. "Because I wanted…"

"What?" He dipped his head to play with her other nipple through the satin of her top.

In his hair, her fingers spread and then clenched again. He licked and laved until the hard little bud was completely defined against the satin. "Tell me what you wanted."

"Do I have to say it?" It was a husky plea that succeeded in capturing his full attention. The second his eyes met hers, he knew. His wife had worn this because she'd wanted to make love. She'd made the first move in her own deliberate way. He'd had no part in seducing her to this point, hadn't even asked for a kiss.

Slowly, he shook his head, almost scared to face the hope bursting to life inside him. "Not this time." Then he grinned, as the hope broke its bonds and shot through his bloodstream like white fire. "We've got years, and I kind of like your way of asking."

Her blush deepened and under his hand, he felt her skin heat up. Looking down, he groaned at the sight of her flushed breast cupped in his palm. The image was rawly sexual and something primitive in him rejoiced. His wife. His woman. His lover.

At last, she was his lover in every sense. Not only accepting but also demanding. And it wasn't just her body she was giving him. The emotions in her eyes were so powerful, he could barely believe it was his composed Victoria in his arms. He still needed to hear the words, needed to see her lips shape them into sound.

If she never said those words, it would hurt but it wouldn't destroy, not when she was willing to show him how much he meant to her in other ways. He kissed his way down to her stomach and along the band of skin exposed by the camisole he'd pushed up. The fingers in his hair tugged.

"Caleb, honey."

He raised his head to glance at her. "Hmm?"

"I want a kiss." Her cheeks were red but the heat wasn't from a blush. The glittering fever in her eyes spoke of something else entirely.

He gave her what she'd asked for. Never would he deny her anything in bed except in sensual play. Vicki's kiss was a stroke of his senses, wild and uninhibited. As she kissed him, she wrapped one leg around his waist and bent the other so that he was cradled against her. The heat passed effortlessly through the satin of her panties and the cotton of his briefs, the most intimate of caresses.

He groaned his pleasure into her mouth, more than willing to let her be the aggressor in this intimacy of lips. Vicki could kiss like no other woman on earth. She put her soul into each glide of the tongue, each sensual bite of the lip until he felt kissed by her whole body.

No one else had ever lavished such pleasure on him.

When she ended the kiss, he gladly let her press him to the bed and straddle his body. She ran her fingers down his chest, through the rough darkness of the hair there. The look in her eyes was hotly sensual, distinctly proprietary.

"What are you doing?" He wasn't complaining. Having his wife's half-naked body for his private viewing pleasure was one of his favorite fantasies.

"Looking at you." She slid the remaining strap of her camisole down her arm. For the first time in their married life there was no shyness in her.

He held his breath as her action bared both breasts. "*Vicki.*"

With a very female smile, she drew the straps off her hands and let the camisole bunch around her waist. Above him, she was a symphony of cream and pink, luscious and tempting. When he ran his hands to her back and pushed gently, she leaned over to let him taste her breasts.

He didn't tug as hard with his teeth as he might have before, aware that her breasts had become more sensitive. Her soft cry of pleasure had him pulling her down enough that he could suckle more of her flesh into his mouth. For long minutes, he alternated between breasts, licking, sucking, laving.

"Wait." She pushed at him until he was flat on his back again, looking up at her.

"Come back," he ordered, his fingers slipping in under the waistband of her panties to stroke her bottom. Her breasts were marked from his caresses, shining wet in the light. The sight was so erotic that he was having a very hard time controlling his arousal.

Instead of obeying, she ran her hands to the waistband of his briefs and slid one inside. Breathing became a lost art. He could barely see through the screaming need tearing through him. Then those slender fingers tightened and his entire body bucked toward her. He managed to keep his eyes open and on her. What he saw stunned him.

Desire lay heavy on her face and her lips were half parted as she breathed in soft gasps. When he groaned, she gave a soft cry. His pleasure fed hers, making him feel more male than he'd ever felt before. "Now, Vicki."

She didn't argue, pulling his briefs down to set his erection free. When she would have moved to take off her panties, he held her in place and, with one hand, simply pushed aside the fabric to bare her.

"*Caleb.*" Her voice held equal measures of shock and hunger.

"Slowly, slowly." He held her back when she would have pushed down hard, not wanting her to hurt herself in spite of the way he craved the silken heat of her body. "That's it, sweetheart. Yeah…just like that." Watching her take him in was so mind-blowing, he had to grit his teeth to stave off his climax.

She arched her back and cried out as she buried him fully within her. She looked like a pagan goddess, a sensual siren far removed from the cool woman he'd once had in his bed.

And then there was no more time to think. She started moving on him in a desperate way that betrayed her own approaching climax. No force on earth could have kept Caleb from shattering moments later, undone by the sensual creature who'd ridden him to ecstasy. He heard Vicki's cry as he went over the edge, a short scream that was worth everything to him.

Ten days after the dinner party that had given him breathing room, Caleb walked out of a highly confidential meeting. He was exhausted but exhilarated. It was almost seven in the evening when he returned to the office but his entire staff was present when he walked in.

The second he stepped out of the elevator, they took one look at him and screamed for joy. The deal had been saved and Callaghan & Associates had showed the business world that when the going got tough, they could step up to the challenge. Caleb knew that the display of grit would gain the firm several new clients as well as reassure their existing ones.

"Let's go celebrate!" someone shouted. There was an immediate round of applause, followed by a rapid discussion of where to go.

"What do you think about that new restaurant-bar on the waterfront?" Kent called out to him.

Caleb raised his hands. "Count me out. I'm heading home."

A chorus of disappointed cries met his words, until Kent winked and said, "Hey, come on now, guys. The man's crazy about his wife."

Caleb laughed along with them. "Enjoy yourselves— put it on the firm's account. Don't worry, I won't take it out of your bonuses."

"I love that word, *bonus*." One of the junior legal clerks did a little jig but Caleb knew his people had more than earned it. He wouldn't forget their dedication.

"Come on, let's get going. Have a good night, Caleb." Excited chatter flowed out of the elevators as they left. He waited until they'd gone before locking up and taking an elevator to the basement garage. He was in a rush to get home.

Because he was crazy about his wife.

Standing there surrounded by people who trusted and respected him, he'd come to the realization that this or any other success would mean nothing if Vicki wasn't there to share it with him. She was the only one who'd ever cared enough about him to be proud of his achievements, the only one who'd ever fought to protect him, the only one…she was, quite simply, the only one.

He could stop running, stop trying to prove himself to Max. The other man no longer mattered. Caleb felt no pain at the thought, just a kind of pity at the self-hatred that had driven Max to alienate a son who would have made him proud. That was too bad for Max but made no difference to Caleb's happiness, because it was rooted in far tougher soil and nurtured by far gentler hands.

He was ready to go home at last.

There was only one more thing he had to do before he left, one step he was finally equipped to take. Using his cell phone, he called Kent's mobile. "Can you meet me for five minutes?"

"Sure, we're not even halfway to the restaurant. I'll walk back up. Something wrong?"

"No." Caleb smiled. "Something's very right."

Caleb walked into the house after ten that night. Tonight of all nights, he hadn't wanted to be late, but fate had conspired against him.

Vicki stepped out of her study, a smile on her face and a pale blue sweater on her slowly thickening body. "Did you get held up at the office?"

He shook his head. "A truck carrying chemicals overturned at one of the major intersections. Traffic was backed up everywhere." Putting his briefcase on the hall table, he pulled off his black wool coat.

Vicki walked over and took it from him. "I'm glad

you're okay." She hung the coat in the closet then hugged him tight. "I missed you."

How had he gotten this lucky? Caleb wondered. "Yeah?"

"Yeah." Her smile grew. "I've been waiting to tell you something."

He pressed her closer, caught by the shining light in her eyes. "What?"

"I got the job. Even though it hasn't been a whole month, they said they want to hire me permanently!" She was almost bursting with excitement. "They were so impressed by that series of radio interviews I lined up that—"

Giving a whoop of delight, Caleb swept her off her feet and swung her around. When he stopped after several revolutions, she was laughing at him, her face flushed with happiness.

"I always knew no one could resist you."

Her grin softened into something unbearably tender. Putting both her hands on his cheeks, she kissed him before sliding down to stand in the circle of his arms. "No wonder I love you so much."

His heart stopped beating. "What did you say?" No one had ever told him that. He couldn't quite believe that Vicki, this woman he adored beyond life, had.

She moved until their faces were a breath away. "I said I love you, Caleb Callaghan. I love you madly, passionately and completely inappropriately. I'm only sorry it took me so long to screw up the guts to say it."

He searched for words to give her in return, trying to find the silver tongue that had led him to the top. "We saved the deal," was what came out.

"Eek! Caleb! Why didn't you say so?" Vicki thumped her fists against his chest. "Why didn't you call?"

"Because I wanted to hold you."

Her joy turned into a smile so lovely, he felt it to the core of his masculinity. "What's the matter?"

"I—I can't find the words."

"The words to say what?"

"How much you mean to me."

"Caleb, honey, I know. *I know.*" She touched his face with a trembling hand. "I listen to you each time you touch me, I finally hear what you say."

It was at that moment that his heart broke wide open. "You are my everything," he whispered, pulling her into a tight embrace. "Don't you ever forget that, and don't you ever let me forget." Without her, he'd be lost, a hollow man with no heart and no soul.

Her arms wrapped around him, her face against his chest. "I'm through with being quiet," she said. "Start getting used to a mouthy wife."

He released her enough to look into her face. "You've been very good about the late nights and the lost weekends."

"The deal was important. I'm not unreasonable. I know your work will sometimes demand those sorts of hours from you. As long as it's not always, I can handle it and so can our child."

"Well, I'll be under far less work stress as of next month." He couldn't believe he'd done it but it felt so right, so perfect. "Callaghan & Associates is about to become Callaghan, Jacobs & Associates."

Vicki's eyes went wide. "You offered Kent a partnership?"

"He's earned it. If I hadn't, I might've lost him to another firm." But that wasn't why he'd done it and it was important to him that she know that. "I don't need to prove myself to anyone anymore." Everything that was important to him was right here in his arms. "All I need is to keep you happy." Vicki had tears in her eyes. He froze. "Honey? What's the matter?"

"I'm so happy." It was a husky whisper. "Oh, Caleb, this means your workload will halve, won't it? I mean, since Kent will have the same responsibilities?"

He smoothed his hand over her hair, trying to stop the tears that always tore him to pieces. "I'll still be the senior partner but yes, Kent is going to start taking over some of my responsibilities, both with files and the management of the firm."

"I'm number one." A tear slid down her cheek. "I never thought I'd be number one no matter how much you loved me."

"I don't und—" Then suddenly he did. "You're the most important thing in my life. Work would mean nothing if you weren't here to come home to. Nothing." He wiped away another fat tear. "Honey, *please.*"

She made a face. "Stupid hormones." Then she hugged him tight, her cheek pressed against his heartbeat. "I think I love you way too much. Can't help it."

He held her and oddly, felt himself start to smile. The smile grew until it creased his entire face. Vicki hated crying because she saw it as a weakness and here she was, sniffling away in his arms. It was as much a declaration of love as the words she'd spoken. "Then cry, honey. I'll always be here to keep you safe. Even if you ever succeed in divorcing me, I'll still be here."

She laughed through the tears. "Idiot. I never wanted to divorce you."

"I know." It had taken him a while but now he understood why she'd done it. "How about a bell?"

"A bell?"

"A really big one."

"Caleb, have you lost your mind?" She shifted to look up at him, a puzzled expression on her face.

"Next time you want my attention, all you have to do is—"

"Ring your bell." She dissolved into laughter. "Caleb!"

He grinned and scooped her up in his arms. "Why don't we go give it a try?" She was perfect—the happy ending he'd never expected from his life. Then she reached up to kiss him and he realized their story was only just beginning.

Epilogue

Caleb watched Vicki at that podium, his heart bursting with pride. She was speaking to an auditorium filled with prospective donors and there was nothing but absolute conviction in her tone. When she finished her presentation, the entire chamber applauded enthusiastically. Even Ada.

Vicki's relationship with her grandmother had changed because Vicki had changed. His wife took no crap from anyone, including him. And he loved her for it. He opened his arms as, with a final smile, the woman at the center of his thoughts walked into the wings and into his embrace. "You were brilliant."

"I was terrified." She grinned.

"It didn't show."

"Where's Hope?"

He pointed behind him to where an adorable three-year-old flirt was trying to talk the stage manager into letting her operate the lights. "She's been charming everyone in sight."

Vicki smiled. "She looks more and more like you every day. Those eyes, that hair—we're going to have to beat off boys with a stick when she starts dating." She ran her fingers through his hair as she spoke.

"Who said my daughter is ever going to date?" He scowled at the very idea.

Vicki laughed softly as they walked to where Hope was standing. When they got to within a few feet of her, she spied them. Giving a shriek, she ran straight into Vicki's arms. "Mommy!"

Caleb knew he shouldn't stand there looking so sappy. It was hardly the image he wanted to present as the senior partner of one of the most successful law firms in town. But there was something magical about seeing his wife's golden head bent over his daughter's dark brown curls.

"What do you want to do tomorrow, muffin?" Vicki asked Hope.

"Sand!" That was Hope's enthusiastic way of saying she'd like to go to the beach.

"Sounds good to me. What about you, honey?" She looked up at him, beautiful, smart and so openly in love with him that he occasionally had to pinch himself to ensure he wasn't dreaming.

"The beach it is." Tomorrow was Saturday. And Saturday and Sunday were for family.

After a few hiccups, they'd eventually managed to find the right work-life balance. When Vicki's position with Heart had started to demand too much, she'd asked Helen for an assistant, something the charities could afford after Vicki's efforts on their behalf.

It had allowed her to be a stay-at-home Mom for Hope

without giving up the intellectual stimulation she thrived on. Rather than losing part of Vicki, Caleb had gained more than he could've imagined. As she grew more self-confident, she seemed to love him more, unafraid to wear her heart on her sleeve.

As for himself, he'd had little trouble delegating most things after Hope's birth. Quite simply, he was fascinated by the tiny creature he'd helped create. He had no intention of missing out on her life. Instead of an absentee father, their Hope was growing up with an overprotective one who loved her to pieces.

But it was Victoria who was the center of his world. Her smile meant more to him than he could ever tell her. It was lucky for him that she could read his love in his every touch. "Hey, beautiful," he said. "You done here?"

"Yes. All I had to do was deliver the speech." She passed Hope to him when their daughter reached for her father, used to having her daddy carry her around. "Spoiled little princess." Vicki laughed as she tickled their child.

Caleb leaned down and kissed his wife's smiling mouth. "I could carry you, too."

Slender fingers tangled into his. "Maybe I'll let you…tonight."

His whole body awakened in anticipation. "I've been thinking. Actually, me and Hope have been having some serious discussions." They usually took place when he drove her to the kindergarten she attended a few mornings a week.

"Uh-huh." It was a suspicious sound as they walked out the exit that led to the parking lot. "What are you two up to?"

Hope snuggled against his shoulder and giggled. Caleb grinned and raised Vicki's hand to his mouth to run his lips along her knuckles.

"Now I'm really suspicious," Vicki said.

"We already have Hope." He caught her gaze. "What do you think about Charity and Mercy?"

Her lips twitched. "Not a chance of our future children having those names. Do you want them teased to death?"

"But yes to the future children?" he murmured.

Standing up on tiptoe, she kissed him. "Definitely. You want a brother or sister, Hope?"

"Yes!" Her cheeks dimpled.

Caleb listened to the sound of his two women talking and felt peace whisper through him. Then Vicki looked at him with those blue eyes and a different, wilder emotion rocked his body and soul. "Everything," he whispered.

You are my everything.

Her smile was jagged with emotion. "Caleb Callaghan, don't you make me cry."

Chuckling, he hugged her to him with one arm, holding his daughter in the other. "Let's go home." So he could love her, adore her, show her exactly what she meant to him.

Everything.

* * * * *

He's proud, passionate, primal—dare
she surrender to the sheikh?

Feel warm winds blowing through your hair
and the hot desert sun on your skin as you are transported
to exotic lands.... As the temperature rises, let yourself be
seduced by our sexy, irresistible sheikhs.

In *Traded to the Sheikh* by Emma Darcy,
Emily Ross is the prisoner of Sheikh Zageo bin
Sultan al Farrahn—he seems to think she'll
trade her body for her freedom! Emily must
prove her innocence before time runs out....

TRADED TO THE SHEIKH

on sale April 2006.

If you enjoyed what you just read,
then we've got an offer you can't resist!

Take 2 bestselling love stories FREE!

Plus get a FREE surprise gift!

Clip this page and mail it to Silhouette Reader Service™

IN U.S.A.
3010 Walden Ave.
P.O. Box 1867
Buffalo, N.Y. 14240-1867

IN CANADA
P.O. Box 609
Fort Erie, Ontario
L2A 5X3

YES! Please send me 2 free Silhouette Desire® novels and my free surprise gift. After receiving them, if I don't wish to receive anymore, I can return the shipping statement marked cancel. If I don't cancel, I will receive 6 brand-new novels every month, before they're available in stores! In the U.S.A., bill me at the bargain price of $3.80 plus 25¢ shipping and handling per book and applicable sales tax, if any*. In Canada, bill me at the bargain price of $4.47 plus 25¢ shipping and handling per book and applicable taxes**. That's the complete price and a savings of at least 10% off the cover prices—what a great deal! I understand that accepting the 2 free books and gift places me under no obligation ever to buy any books. I can always return a shipment and cancel at any time. Even if I never buy another book from Silhouette, the 2 free books and gift are mine to keep forever.

225 SDN DZ9F
326 SDN DZ9G

Name	(PLEASE PRINT)	
Address	Apt.#	
City	State/Prov.	Zip/Postal Code

Not valid to current Silhouette Desire® subscribers.

Want to try two free books from another series?
Call 1-800-873-8635 or visit www.morefreebooks.com.

* Terms and prices subject to change without notice. Sales tax applicable in N.Y.
** Canadian residents will be charged applicable provincial taxes and GST.
   All orders subject to approval. Offer limited to one per household.
   ® are registered trademarks owned and used by the trademark owner and or its licensee.

DES04R   ©2004 Harlequin Enterprises Limited

It's a
SUMMER OF SECRETS

Expecting
Lonergan's Baby

(#1719)

by

MAUREEN CHILD

He'd returned only for the summer...until a
passionate encounter with a sensual stranger
has this Lonergan bachelor contemplating
forever...and fatherhood.

**Don't miss the SUMMER OF SECRETS trilogy,
beginning in April from Silhouette Desire.**

On sale April 2006
Available at your favorite retail outlet!

Silhouette® *Desire*

COMING NEXT MONTH

#1717 THE FORBIDDEN TWIN—Susan Crosby
The Elliotts
Seducing your twin sister's ex-fiancé by pretending to be her...
not the best idea. Unless he succumbs.

**#1718 THE TEXAN'S FORBIDDEN AFFAIR—
Peggy Moreland**
A Piece of Texas
He swept her off her feet, then destroyed her. Now he wants her
back!

**#1719 EXPECTING LONERGAN'S BABY—
Maureen Child**
Summer of Secrets
He was home just for the summer—until a night of explosive
passion gave him a reason to stay.

**#1720 THEIR MILLION-DOLLAR NIGHT—
Katherine Garbera**
What Happens in Vegas...
This businessman has millions at stake in a deal but one woman
has him risking scandal and damning the consequences!

#1721 BABY, I'M YOURS—Catherine Mann
It was only supposed to be a weekend affair, then an unexpected
pregnancy changed all of the rules.

**#1722 THE SOLDIER'S SEDUCTION—
Anne Marie Winston**
She thought the man who'd taken her innocence was gone
forever...until he returned home to claim her—and the daughter
he never knew existed.

SDCNM0306